ROM
F
CAR

8903418

17.95

Cartland, Barbara
A game of love

A GAME OF LOVE

The Earl of Inchester comes to London in despair.

After returning from fighting gallantly in France against Napoleon he has tried for three years to save his ancestral home and his estate.

To do so he is forced to borrow money from Rustuss Groon, the most notorious Usurer in the whole of London.

He has returned now for the second time to beg him on his knees to lend him more.

Rustuss Groon, who is a ghastly-looking old man with black hair and dark glasses sitting in a dingy office off Piccadilly, says he will help him on one condition, that he will marry his daughter.

The Earl is appalled at the idea, knowing his ancestors would never forgive him for despoiling the dignity and pride of the family.

However, in order to save his pensioners who are practically suffering from starvation, he agrees.

Rustuss Groon has everything arranged for the wedding to take place the following day in a Private Chapel.

How the Earl arrives at the Chapel feeling he is going to the guillotine and how, strangely enough, his bride has exactly the same feeling.

How later they meet each other by chance and find everything very different from what they expected.

How the beautiful Benita saves the Earl's life in a duel and falls in love is all told in this unusual and exciting 443rd book by Barbara Cartland.

A GAME OF LOVE

Barbara Cartland

SEVERN HOUSE PUBLISHERS

IC

This first world edition published in 1990 by
SEVERN HOUSE PUBLISHERS LTD of
35 Manor Road, Wallington, Surrey SM6 0BW.
Simultaneously published in the U.S.A. by
SEVERN HOUSE PUBLISHERS INC., NEW YORK

British Library Cataloguing in Publication Data
Cartland, Barbara *1902–*
  A game of love.
  I. Title
  823'.912 [F]

ISBN 0-7278-1769-8

Distributed in the U.S.A. by
Mercedes Distribution Center, Inc.
62 Imlay Street, Brooklyn, N.Y. 11231

Printed and bound in Great Britain
at the University Press, Cambridge

AUTHOR'S NOTE

There were a number of proprietory or Private Chapels in London during the 17th and 18th Centuries.

They were most of them built by private speculators more as a means of profit than of spiritual welfare.

They were not consecrated but empowered to perform 'First Marriages' which means that no Licence, Banns or Paternal Consent was required.

The marriages were perfectly legal, but expensive, and the Chapels attracted large congregations by offering either exciting Preachers or good music.

The Mayfair Chapel in London was one of the best known.

The Duke of Hamilton met Elizabeth Gunning at Lord Chesterfield's home in 1752. Two nights later he sent for a Parson to marry them.

The Clergyman refused without the proper papers.

The Duke then took Elizabeth to the Mayfair Chapel where they were married with a ring off a bed curtain at half-past twelve at night.

There was the Berkeley Chapel and various other Chapels, and the average salary for a Preacher at this time was £50 a year.

The Chapels, because they were privately owned, were very much more comfortable than the orthodox Churches.

The Berkeley Chapel was upholstered throughout with pink velvet, and heavy hangings on brass rods.

ABOUT THE AUTHOR

Barbara Cartland, the world's most famous romantic novelist, who is also an historian, playwright, lecturer, political speaker and television personality, has now written over 460 books and sold nearly 500 million copies all over the world.

She has also had many historical works published and has written four autobiographies as well as the biographies of her mother and that of her brother, Ronald Cartland, who was the first Member of Parliament to be killed in the last war. This book has a preface by Sir Winston Churchill and has just been republished with an introduction by the late Sir Arthur Bryant.

"Love at the Helm" a novel written with the help and inspiration of the late Earl Mountbatten of Burma, Great Uncle of His Royal Highness The Prince of Wales, is being sold for the Mountbatten Memorial Trust.

She has broken the world record for the last twelve years by writing an average of twenty-three books a year. In the Guinness Book of Records she is listed as the world's top-selling author.

Miss Cartland in 1978 sang an Album of Love Songs with the Royal Philharmonic Orchestra.

In private life Barbara Cartland, who is a Dame of Grace of the Order of St. John of Jerusalem, Chairman of the St. John Council in Hertfordshire and Deputy President of the St. John Ambulance Brigade, has fought for better conditions and salaries for Midwives and Nurses.

She championed the cause for the Elderly in 1956 invoking a Government Enquiry into the "Housing Conditions of Old People".

In 1962 she had the Law of England changed so that Local Authorities had to provide camps for their own Gypsies. This has meant that since then thousands and thousands of Gypsy children have been able to go to School which they had never been able to do in the past, as their caravans were moved every twenty-four hours by the Police.

There are now fourteen camps in Hertfordshire and Barbara Cartland has her own Romany Gypsy Camp called Barbaraville by the Gypsies.

Her designs "Decorating with Love" are being sold all over the U.S.A. and the National Home Fashions League made her, in 1981, "Woman of Achievement".

Barbara Cartland's book "Getting Older, Growing Younger" has been published in Great Britain and the U.S.A. and her fifth Cookery Book, ""The Romance of Food", is now being used by the House of Commons.

In 1984 she received at Kennedy Airport, America's Bishop Wright Air Industry Award for her contribution to the development of aviation. In 1931 she and two R.A.F. Officers thought of, and carried, the first aeroplane-towed glider air-mail.

During the War she was Chief Lady Welfare Officer in Bedfordshire looking after 20,000 Service men and women. She thought of having a pool of Wedding Dresses at the War Office so a Service Bride could hire a gown for the day.

She bought 1,000 gowns without coupons for the A.T.S., the W.A.A.F.s and the W.R.E.N.S. In 1945 Barbara Cartland received the Certificate of Merit from Eastern Command.

In 1964 Barbara Cartland founded the National Association for Health of which she is the President, as a front for all the Health Stores and for any product made as alternative medicine.

This has now a £500,000,000 turnover a year, with one third going in export.

In January 1988 she received "La Medaille de Vermeil de la Ville de Paris", (the Gold Medal of Paris). This is the highest award to be given by the City of Paris for ACHIEVEMENT – 25 million books sold in France.

In March 1988 Barbara Cartland was asked by the Indian Government to open their Health Resort outside Delhi. This is almost the largest Health Resort in the world.

Barbara Cartland was received with great enthusiasm by her fans, who also fêted her at a Reception in the city and she received the gift of an embossed plate from the Government.

OTHER BOOKS BY
BARBARA CARTLAND

Romantic Novels, over 400, the most recently published being:

A Kiss From A Stranger	The Wrong Duchess
A Very Special Love	The Taming of a Tigress
A Necklace of Love	Loves Comes To The Castle
A Revolution of Love	The Magic of Paris

The Marquis Wins
Love is the Key
Free as the Wind
Desire in the Desert
A Heart in the Highlands
The Music of Love

Stand and Deliver Your Heart
The Scent of Roses
Love at First Sight
The Secret Princess
Heaven in Hong Kong
Paradise in Penang

The Dream and the Glory (In aid of the St. John Ambulance Brigade)

Autobiographical and Biographical:

The Isthmus Years 1919-1939
The Years of Opportunity 1939-1945
I Search for Rainbows 1945-1976
We Danced All Night 1919-1929
Ronald Cartland (With a foreword by Sir Winston Churchill)
Polly – My Wonderful Mother
I Seek the Miraculous

Historical:

Bewitching Women
The Outrageous Queen (The Story of Queen Christina of Sweden)
The Scandalous Life of King Carol
The Private Life of Charles II
The Private Life of Elizabeth, Empress of Austria
Josephine, Empress of France
Diane de Poitiers
Metternich – The Passionate Diplomat

Sociology:

You in the Home
The Fascinating Forties
Marriage for Moderns
Be Vivid, Be Vital
Love, Life and Sex
Vitamins for Vitality
Husbands and Wives
Men are Wonderful

Etiquette
The Many Facets of Love
Sex and the Teenager
The Book of Charm
Living Together
The Youth Secret
The Magic of Honey
The Book of Beauty and
Health

Keep Young and Beautiful by Barbara Cartland and Elinor
Glyn
Etiquette for Love and Romance
Barbara Cartland's Book of Health

General

Barbara Cartland's Book of Useless Information with a
Foreword by the Earl Mountbatten of Burma.
(In aid of the United World College)
Love and Lovers (Picture Book)
The Light of Love (Prayer Book)
Barbara Cartland's Scrapbook
(In aid of the Royal Photographic Museum)
Romantic Royal Marriages
Barbara Cartland's Book of Celebrities
Getting Older, Growing Younger

Verse:

Lines on Life and Love

Music:

An Album of Love Songs sung with the Royal Philharmonic Orchestra.

Films

The Flame is Love
A Hazard of Hearts

Cartoons:

Barbara Cartland's Romances (Book of Cartoons) has recently been published in the U.S.A., Great Britain, and other parts of the world.

Children:

A Children's Pop-Up Book: "Princess to the Rescue"

Cookery

Barbara Cartland's Health Food Cookery Book
Food for Love
Magic of Honey Cookbook
Recipes for Lovers
The Romance of Food

Editor of:

"The Common Problem" by Ronald Cartland (with a preface by the Rt. Hon. the Earl of Selborne, P.C.)

Barbara Cartland's Library of Love
                        Library of Ancient Wisdom
"Written with Love" Passionate love letters selected by
    Barbara Cartland

Drama:

Blood Money
French Dressing

Philosophy:

Touch the Stars

Radio Operetta:

The Rose and the Violet (Music by Mark Lubbock) Per-
    formed in 1942.

Radio Plays:

The Caged Bird: An episode in the life of Elizabeth
    Empress of Austria. Performed in 1957.

CHAPTER ONE

1818

The Earl of Inchester walked into White's Club.

As he entered the Morning Room he thought he was stepping back into the past.

He almost expected to see Beau Brummell sitting in his usual seat in the bow-window.

But Beau Brummell had been exiled to the Continent two years earlier, and he looked round for a familiar face.

Then somebody exclaimed:

"Inchester!"

He saw his friend Sir Anthony Keswick at the end of the room.

He walked across to join him and Sir Anthony exclaimed:

"You are a stranger, Garth! I thought we had lost you for ever!"

The Earl smiled slightly and sat down beside him.

"I am alive," he said, "but only just!"

"Are things bad?" his friend asked.

"Very!"

"Then have a drink."

"Only if you pay for it," the Earl replied.

"As bad as that?"

"Worse!"

Sir Anthony called to a steward and ordered a bottle of champagne.

"I can see you need cheering up," he said. "What has happened?"

"I am not going to tell you," the Earl said, "because it is so depressing. I have failed, Tony, failed completely in everything I have tried to do."

"I cannot believe it!" Sir Anthony exclaimed.

The Earl sighed.

"I have come to London to seek one last chance of saving myself, and if this fails I might as well blow a piece of lead through my brains!"

The steward opened the champagne.

Sir Anthony put a glass into his friend's hand and picked up one for himself.

"I am going to propose a toast that is also a prediction," he said, "that things will be better for you in the future!"

"I can only pray you are right," the Earl answered.

As he sipped the champagne he looked round.

There were some new faces and quite a number of the old ones.

They were all drinking, all perfectly at their ease despite all the suffering during and after the War.

He could see the Duke of Norfolk.

As usual he was drinking an inordinate amount and managing to watch every one of his friends collapse before he did.

The Duke, who was known as Jockey Norfolk, was a

man who could drink from noon until the following dawn and still be on his feet.

It was an achievement in itself.

The hard drinkers of St. James's Street were notorious for managing bottle after bottle before they eventually disappeared under the table.

Norfolk was certainly a personality.

At the Beefsteak Club he would consume five rump-steaks at a sitting and several bottles of port.

There were dozens of tales told about him and the Earl turned his head away in disgust.

He was thinking that such drinking was an abominable extravagance which few men of his age could really afford.

The expression on his face made Sir Anthony say:

"Let me lend you 'a monkey'."

The Earl shook his head.

"Thank you, Tony. You have always been a good friend, but I am not sponging on you or anybody else."

Sir Anthony looked at him questioningly.

"You are not going to the Usurers?"

There was no need for the Earl to answer.

"You cannot do that!" Sir Anthony exclaimed. "I have seen too many sucked dry and left with nothing but their lives."

"That is more or less my position," the Earl said bitterly.

As he spoke he knew it was the aftermath of War.

In some the peace was even more terrible than the actual fighting had been against Napoleon's 'Invincible' Army.

It was one thing to suffer danger on the field of battle, and to believe that by pitting your wits against your enemy you were defending your country and being a hero.

It was quite another to return to find your home in state

of dilapidation, with the roof and ceilings falling in, and with the fields unplanted and uncropped, because the able-bodied men had gone to War.

Then to learn, as had happened in the last two years, that country Banks were closing their doors.

That Farmers were bankrupt because there was no market for what they did grow.

It was difficult, the Earl thought, for anyone like himself not to feel bitter.

Especially when he saw men who had served with unquestionable bravery being demobolised without a pension or a gratuity and without a word of thanks.

He finished off his champagne and Sir Anthony refilled his glass.

"What are you going to do, Garth?" he asked quietly.

"I am going to crawl on my knees," the Earl said in a harsh voice, "to Rustuss Groon."

His friend gave an exclamation of horror.

"Not Rustuss Groon! Do not tell me you have been to that shark. You must be crazy!"

"Two years ago, when nobody else would lend me a penny he obliged."

"Then all I can say is I would rather throw myself into the sea than try to borrow from the hardest-hearted usurer that ever had an office in the West End!"

The Earl did not reply, and after a moment Sir Anthony said:

"Surely you have something left to sell?"

"I have sold all I can," the Earl replied. "The money went to pay the bills that accrued when my mother was desperately ill. Everything now left in the house is entailed onto the son I can never afford to have!"

"What about your land? You have a considerable number of acres?"

"They are full of weeds and hardly any have been ploughed. Even if they were, I cannot afford the seed to put into the ground."

Sir Anthony sighed,

"I am desperately sorry for you, Garth."

"I am sorry for myself," the Earl replied, "and even more for my pensioners. They are hungry, Tony! Can you imagine what it is like to know that people who have served my family for generations are hungry, and I am unable to help them?"

There was a sound almost of agony in the Earl's voice.

Sir Anthony filled up his glass obviously unable to find words with which to comfort him.

They sat in silence for a little while, then Sir Anthony asked:

"Are you really going to see that man?"

"I have an appointment for five o'clock."

"An appointment?"

"I wrote to him asking if I could see him. I knew it would be a waste of money to come to London if he did not happen to be here."

"He will be here if he can pluck naked some fool who is having a run of bad luck."

Sir Anthony spoke scornfully, and the Earl said:

"I had a reply telling me to call to-day. I have been praying all the way here that he has not decided to require me to return what I have already borrowed."

"I would not want you to be too optimistic," Sir Anthony murmured. "Bradford had to leave for the Continent last year, and it is unlikely he will ever be able to afford to come back."

The Earl looked at his friend in surprise.

"I thought he was 'warm in the pocket'!"

"He was until he started to gamble at the high table and

borrow from Rustuss Groon to pay his losses."

"You mean he had nothing left?"

"Nothing except for an ancestral home which was falling about his ears, and land which is in a state of rack and ruin."

The Earl drew in his breath as he knew he was in the same boat.

He poured what was left in his glass down his throat and rose to his feet.

"It is not yet five o'clock,' Sir Anthony said.

"I know," the Earl replied, "but in dealing with Rustuss Groon I need to have my wits about me. So I dare not drink any more."

"If he is more obliging that you anticipate," Sir Anthony said, "come back and we will go on the Town. There are some very alluring new Cyprians, or we can drop in on Harriet Wilson."

"Good Heavens!" the Earl exclaimed. "I had nearly forgotten she existed."

"She would not be flattered! She has a Peer or two in tow, including the Duke of Wellington, and her sister Amy who is even cleverer that she is has actually married the Duke of Berwick."

"I can hardly believe it!" the Earl exclaimed.

Harriet Wilson and her three sisters, Amy, Fanny and Sophia were four of the best-known Cyprians in London.

They were the daughters of a man called Debouchet, a clock-maker.

He was said to be the off-spring of a union between the Earl of Chesterfield and a Continental *limoadiere*.

Their mother, who made silk stockings, was also illegitimate.

All the sisters led very colourful and notorious lives.

Harriet made no secret of the fact that she had become

the mistress of the Earl of Craven at the age of fifteen.

She had then lived under the protection of a succession of older, important aristocrats.

She was writing her Memoirs.

A large number of one-time dashing young *Beaux,* who had become more respectable as they grew older, were extremely nervous as to how they would figure in it.

The Earl smiled before he replied:

"I do not think I would grace to-night the sort of parties that Harriet gives. Whichever way my conversation with Groon goes, I shall return to the country."

"It is fortunate you do not live far from London," his friend remarked. "Beware of Highwaymen!"

The Earl laughed.

"Any Highwayman who gets anything out of me would be a magician. In fact I have often thought of taking to the road myself!"

"It is not a bad idea," Sir Anthony said, "except that if you are caught, it would be damned uncomfortable dangling from a rope!"

"You are right there," the Earl agreed. "Good-bye, Tony, and thank you for the champagne."

"I will have another bottle waiting in case you come back," Sir Anthony said.

The Earl shook his head and walked towards the door.

He was a remarkably good-looking young man.

Quite a number of the members seated in the leather arm-chairs looked at him as he passed by.

He had a fine physique with broad shoulders and narrow hips giving him an athletic appearance.

Many men of the same age could not help envying him.

"Good-night, M'Lord!" the Porter said respectfully as he opened the door for the Earl. "Nice to see your Lordship again!"

"Thank you, Jenkins," the Earl replied. "Good-night."

There was a cold wind blowing down St. James's Street.

The Earl started to walk up it and felt it biting into his bones.

He had left his overcoat, because it was so dilapidated, where he had stabled his horse.

He wished now he had kept it with him.

As he reached Piccadilly he started to pray that Rustuss Groon would help.

Otherwise he had not the slightest idea what he could do.

In one of the narrow streets running off Piccadilly as it neared the Circus there was a dark door up three steps.

They belonged to a small house squeezed between two larger ones.

There was nothing to distinguish it except for the knocker of the door which needed polishing.

A small plaque lay beneath it on which was engraved:

RUSTUSS GROON

USURER

Inside was a narrow passage with uncarpeted stairs leading up to the floor above.

On the left there was a small dingy office which seemed almost filled by a huge desk.

The walls were dark and the 'curtains', which was a polite name for them, were drawn over the dirty window.

The only light came from two candles at each end of the desk on which there was an ink-pot fashioned out of a skull.

There was also a jam-jar in which were inserted a number of quill pens.

Seated at the desk there appeared to be an elderly man with untidy black hair which fell each side of his face.

His eyes were concealed behind dark glasses.

Although those sitting opposite him could not see his expression through them, they were uncomfortably aware that he was watching them.

He appeared to look deeply into their very characters.

"The man frightens me!" one *Beau* had said to Sir Anthony. "There is something uncanny about him, and I swear he reads one's thoughts!"

"I would not be surprised," Sir Anthony said. "I have never been to the man, thank God, but everyone who does so says the same, that he is either clairvoyant or a Witch Doctor!"

"If I had my way he would hang for it!" the *Beau* said furiously.

"Then you would be fool enough to go to another of his kind," Sir Anthony said. "Why can you not keep your money in your pocket instead of throwing it down the drain?"

Because he was not receiving any sympathy the *Beau* walked away.

Sir Anthony thought he must be right about Rustuss Groon.

He was uncanny, and very much more astute than the ordinary Moneylender.

Now Rustuss Groon said in a deep but surprisingly educated voice:

"I think, Dawson, we have let the Marquess 'cool his heels' long enough to make him apprehensive."

Dawson, the man to whom Rustuss Groon had spoken, rose from his desk in the next room.

It was almost identical, if sightly smaller, and came to the communicating-door.

"Do you have the report on the Marquess?" he asked.

"Yes, I have it in front of me," Rustuss Groon replied. "He spent everything I lent him on women and drink! Women who came from 'the Coal Hob' on 'Tiger Bay' and the drink he has consumed would fill a lake!"

"If you ask me," Dawson said, "he is a nasty piece of work without a redeeming feature."

"I agree with you," Mr Groon answered. "At the same time, he is a Marquess!"

Dawson did not answer and for the moment his employer seemed to be deep in thought.

Then he said sharply:

"Bring him in!"

Dawson left the room and crossed the passage to where there was another room hardly bigger than a cupboard.

It looked out into a dirty yard at the back of the building.

At thirty-three the Marquess should have been at his best.

But years of debauchery and staying up late night after night in the Night-Clubs, the Drinking-Taverns and the Gaming-Rooms had taken their toll.

He was overweight, his face was red and puffy.

The lines were deeply etched under his eyes and the eyes themselves were sunken into his head.

He had a heavy paunch.

When Dawson appeared it was with some difficulty that he got out of the chair in which he had been sitting.

"It is about time!" he said testily. "I thought your Master must have forgotten about me!"

"He is ready for you now, M'Lord," Dawson said.

He walked ahead to open the door into the office.

With an effort the Marquess straightened his shoulders and lifted his chin.

He walked in, but Rustuss Groon did not raise his head from what he was reading.

In fact, if anything, he seemed to crouch a litle lower.

In the flickering light of the two candles his back seemed to have a hunch on it.

"You have kept me waiting a long time!" the Marquess said in a lofty tone.

"Sit down!" Rustuss Groon spoke in an even deeper voice than the one he had used to Dawson.

There seemed something menacing about it.

The Marquess seated himself on the hard-backed chair which stood in front of his desk.

Then he began

"Now, look here! I need another loan and I think the interest you charged me on the last one was exorbitant!"

He paused for Rustuss Groon to speak, and when he did not do so, the Marquess went on:

"I am prepared to offer you 20% and not a penny more – do you understand?"

Rustuss Groon raised his head.

"I am not prepared, my Lord Marquess, to lend you any more money, and I want what I have already lent you returned immediately!"

There was a heavy silence while the Marquess stared at him.

Then such an expression of horror came on his face that it seemed as if his eyes might drop out of their sockets.

"You – want the return – of your £30,000?"

"Immediately!"

"But – you know as well as I do that I – cannot find – £30,000!"

"Then you have two alternatives."

There was an uncomfortable silence until the Marquess asked in a lower voice than he had used previously:

"What – are they?"

"You can go to the Debtors' Prison in the Fleet, or you can sign this paper."

"Sign – what paper? What does it say?" the Marquess demanded.

"It is a Deed making over to me the five-hundred acres of land on the South side of your Park which include the village of Lower Rowden and also the Slate Mine."

The Marquess stared at him.

He appeared for the moment to be completely speechless.

Then he said quickly:

"That land is entailed."

"That is not true, My Lord,' Rustuss Groon replied, "so do not waste my time lying about it. That land was added to the estate when your mother married your father. It also includes the Dower House which is in passable repair compared to Rowden Hall."

The Marquess gave a cry that was almost a screech.

"How do you know that? How the devil do you know all these things about me?"

"I have made enquiries," Rustuss Groon replied, "and I have no intention, My Lord, of throwing good money after bad."

He paused and then continued:

"When I made you a loan of £30,000 you told me you intended to repair your house, put your land into cultivation, and employ men coming out of the Armed Services who were badly in need of work. You have done none of these things!"

The Marquess bowed his head.

Then he said:

"London is cursed expensive, and the money was not enough."

"You need not go into details as to how you spent it," Rustuss Groon said. "A ruby necklace given to a Bit O'Muslin is hardly the same as cultivating your crops, or making your Slate Mine productive."

"What do you mean by poking your nose into my affairs?" the Marquess shouted. "What I do with my money is my business!"

"It is *my* money," Rustuss Groon reminded him, "and that is why, My Lord, you will sign this paper, or take the consequences."

There was a long silence.

Then as if the Marquess realised he was beaten he stared down at the paper.

Rustuss Groon had pushed it across the desk towards him.

Silently he picked up a quill pen.

His hand was shaking as he held it for a moment poised over the paper.

Then as he signed his name he exclaimed:

"Damn you! Curse you! May you rot in Hell where undoubtedly you belong!"

Rustuss Groon did not appear to hear the abuse.

He merely reached over and picked up the piece of paper.

He studied it as if to make sure that the signature was correct.

He was well aware that the Marquess, standing staring down at him, was contemplating whether or not he would strike him.

Finally he walked towards the door.

Dawson opened it for him.

Before he went through it, the Marquess turned to look back at Rustuss Groon.

"You are the Devil himself – that is what you are – the Devil! I hope you burn in your own Hell-fire!"

He walked towards the outer door, opened it and slammed it shut behind him.

Dawson shut the door of the office and went to his master's desk.

"It might have been worse," he remarked, laconically.

"You can tell Coombe that the Slate Mine is now in our possession," Rustuss Groon said, "and remind him to keep his promise, first to pay the pensioners and see to their houses."

Dawson nodded.

"He is a decent man, and I am sure you will not regret letting him buy it."

"We have made only a small profit by selling to Coombe," Rustuss Groon replied, "but I did not trust that other man."

"Nor did I," Dawson agreed. "He might have worked the Slate Mine well enough, but I do not think he would have been interested in the village or the people in it."

"That is what I thought myself," Rustuss Groon agreed. "Now – who is next?"

"The Earl of Inchester."

"Yes, of course."

"Here are the papers about him," Dawson said bringing them from his desk. " The last man we employed is, I think, excellent! He finds out things which I would have thought were beyond his capabilities."

"I told him to let me have every possible particular," Rustuss Groon said in a low voice as if he was speaking to himself.

Dawson was glancing at the clock on the mantlepiece beneath which there was no fire.

It was cold in the office, and both he and Rustuss

Groon were wearing their overcoats.

"I hope the Earl is not going to be late." the latter said. "I want to go home."

"Are you in pain?" Dawson asked sympathetically.

"Yes."

The monosyllable was uttered reluctantly.

"Shall I get your drops?" Dawson offered.

There was a pause before Rustuss Groon replied:

"Perhaps you had better."

Dawson opened a drawer in the desk and brought out a bottle.

Very carefully he poured three drops into a glass, added a little water and handed it to his Master.

Rustuss Groon swallowed it.

Then he sat back as if it coursed through his throat and down to his chest.

As he did so there was a 'rat-tat' on the front-door.

Dawson put the bottle back into the drawer.

"Shall I bring His Lordship in, or make him wait?"

"Bring him in," Rustuss Groon ordered.

The Earl came into the office.

After the Marquess, his clear complexion and his slim body, made him seem like someone from another planet.

"Good-afternoon!" he said to the Usurer.

He had taken off his hat as he came into the house.

The Marquess, to show his superiority, had kept his on.

"Sit down, My Lord," Rustuss Groon said.

The Earl did so, putting his tall hat upside-down on the floor beside him.

"I wrote to you," he said after drawing in a deep breath, "because I am in trouble."

There was no reply from the man to whom he was speaking who once again seemed to be sunk lower into the desk.

At the same time, behind the dark-coloured spectacles he was obviously watching the Earl.

"I have tried," the Earl said. "I swear I have tried in every possible way to make things work and get things going. But I have failed! I admit I have failed completely!"

Rustuss Groon did not speak, and he went on:

"It has got worse and worse, and last year proved a complete disaster for all Farmers."

He paused to take a deep breath and then continued:

"The weather was against us, our crops failed one after another, and there was not the demand, in the markets, for what we did grow which we had expected there to be."

His voice was bitter as he went on:

"I understand cheap food is being imported into this country from abroad. Our Farmers were encouraged to grow more and to expend more money, time and energy on the land during the War. Now nobody is interested, and there are no jobs for the men who are leaving the Forces."

"I am aware of that," Rustuss Groon said. "However it is you I am interested in, My Lord, and not in the Farming community as a whole."

"Then I can only be honest and tell you I have spent every penny you lent me in trying to pull my estate together. You are welcome, if you wish, to see the accounts, and I can only assure you that nothing has been spent on riotous living."

He drew in his breath before he went on:

"I am praying that we shall have a decent lambing season this year. But the ewes have not been fed as well as they should, and without the right food my cows cannot give milk."

There was a note of despair in the Earl's voice as he looked at the man to whom he was speaking.

He made a gesture with his hands that was very elo-
quent before he sat back as if he needed the support of the
chair behind him.

There was a long silence before Rustuss Groon in his
low hoarse voice spoke.

"I am well aware, My Lord, that you have told me the
truth."

"But how would you know that?" the Earl asked.

"I have my methods of knowing most things," Rustuss
Groon replied. "I know that you yourself have worked
long and late, and because you inspire respect the men
who serve you have done the same without complaint."

"Loyalty, as we found in the Army," the Earl said, "does
not fill an empty belly."

Rustuss Groon nodded his head.

Then as he did not speak the Earl reminded him:

"When you replied to my letter you said you had a
proposition to put to me."

"That is true," Rustuss Groon agreed, "and I want you
to consider it very carefully."

"You know I would do anything – anything – to help
my people."

"What I am going to suggest," Rustuss Groon said,
"will enable you to repair your house, improve your estate, plan the right crops, and replenish your sheep and
cattle."

The Earl sat upright in his chair and stared at the man
opposite him.

"I can do that?" he asked in an astonished tone. "But –
how?"

"You may not like my suggestions, and of course you
are at liberty to refuse," Rustuss Groon said, "and con-
tinue to owe me £20,000."

The Earl was well aware of the threat implied, and he

would have been very stupid not to realise it.

He could either agree to whatever the Usurer suggested, or there would be no more money available for him.

He also knew that one day – God knew how – he would have to repay him the money he had borrowed originally.

For a moment he was afraid.

Then he told himself that if he could face Napoleon he would not cringe before Rustuss Groon.

With an effort he managed to say:

"Of course I am only too willing to listen to anything you may propose, and will naturally give it my most serious consideration."

"What I am suggesting is quite simple," Rustuss Groon said. "It is, My Lord, that you should marry my daughter!"

For a moment the world seemed to have stopped turning, the clock ticking.

The Earl just stared in disbelief at the man on the opposite side of the desk.

Then in a voice that did not sound like his own he asked:

"Did you say – I should – marry your – daughter?"

"That is what I said," Rustuss Groon said. "Let me explain."

The Earl was still staring at him as if he could not believe what he had heard.

"I am a very rich man, but I have only one child, my daughter, who will inherit everything I posess."

There was a long pause before he continued:

"I wish her to be married to a man I can trust not to throw her money away on cards, drink and 'Cyprians'. That is why I have chosen you as her husband."

The Earl could not believe his ears.

It flashed through his mind that his family went back to before the Norman Conquest.

The first Earl of Inchester received the title for gallantry at the Battle of Agincourt.

Each succeeding Monarch had been served by his ancestors, and both his grand-father and his father had distinguished themselves as soldiers.

His ancestor had been one of Marlborough's most trusted Generals.

His father had commanded the Household Cavalry.

He felt as if he could see their faces looking down at him from their portraits which hung on the walls of Inch.

Beside many of them were the beautiful women they had married and whose blood had equalled that of Chesters.

They had been painted by the great artists of their time, and he could see their face clearly.

Their straight, aristocratic noses, their clear English complexions.

Their eyes seeming to look innocently out of their portraits.

They knew nothing of the sordid horrors that lay beneath the surface of every period of history.

They were the mothers of fine children.

Of tall, handsome men like his father, and beautiful women like his mother.

They married into the Peerage and were traditionally in attendance upon the Queen as Ladies-of-the-Bedchamber.

It struck him almost like a blow.

If he introduced amongst them the daughter of the man facing him, her blood might change the family characteristics which had been inherited by generation after generation.

The men would be dark instead of fair, their character cunning instead of innocent, crafty instead of gracious.

"How can I do it? In God's name, how can I do such a thing?" he wanted to ask.

Then, the self-control he had been taught ever since he was a small boy kept him silent.

He could only feel as if his brain was turning, turning round and round on wheels.

It was impossible for him to make a decision – impossible for him to answer.

"How could I marry *your* daughter?" he wanted to ask.

Then as he shrunk from the idea, he saw instead of the faces of his ancestors, those of the old pensioners.

He was well aware when he visited their leaking, creaking cottages that they had become emaciated, through penury.

He knew their eyes were pleading with him to take pity on them.

There were so many of them.

His father had always been a rich man.

There had been at least thirty servants employed at the 'Big House'.

There were Gardeners, Game-Keepers, Carpenters, Stone-Masons, Brick-Layers, Wheelwrights and Black-smiths employed on the estate.

He could remember his father saying to him once when he was a small boy:

"We have nearly a thousand people to pay every Friday. As you grow older, Garth, you will understand we are a state within a state. These are our people, and neither you nor I must ever forsake or neglect them."

It was because of the pensioners that he had gone to Rustuss Groon.

It was also because a number of them and the Farmers

had sons who had now come home after fighting the French.

Some had been left behind.

They were in hurriedly dug graves.

Only a rough wooden cross pressed into the ground indicated where a young man lay.

They had fought to keep England free and now would no longer suffer.

But what of their brothers, their cousins, their friends, their contemporaries?

Were they to sit about and starve because there was no work?

No money to pay them if they did?

"What am I to do? Oh, God, what am I to do?" the Earl asked himself.

Without really thinking what he was doing, he rose from the chair and walked to the window.

He pulled back the filthy piece of rag which served as a curtain and looked out.

It was dusk outside and the dark shadows in the street were sinister.

An old man came shuffling along.

He was obviously battling against the force of the wind to keep on his feet.

It was a struggle for him to put one foot before another.

His clothes were ragged, and he wore a scarf around his neck in an effort to keep warm.

To the Earl he typified everything that was happening in his vilage and on his estate.

Old people were suffering through no fault of their own.

He could save them, and how could he refuse to do so?

He turned round.

Rustuss Groon had not moved.

He had not even turned his head to follow him with his eyes.

He just sat, waiting.

The Earl knew he had no alternative.

"Very well," he said at last in a hard voice. "I will marry your daughter!"

CHAPTER TWO

Riding back over ground still sparkling with frost, Benita Grenfel thought she was very happy.

She loved the frosty mornings when the ground was white and the trees were sparkling in the sunshine.

In a very short time the first snowdrops would appear.

Then there would be buds on every bough and it would be Spring.

"I love the country," she said to herself. "If only Papa could be with me and not keep having to go to London."

It was wonderful to have him with her at the end of the week, but she knew he was not well.

He could no longer ride with her as he used to do.

He had taught her to ride when she was very small.

She had found no difficulty during the last few years when he could afford superb horses.

She could ride the more spirited animals just as well as she had ridden the ordinary hacks which, in her childhood, was all they had been able to afford.

Somehow, although she thought it was wrong, it had

been a blessing in disguise when her father had been wounded.

He had been sent home from Portugal.

Her mother had nursed him back to comparatively good health again.

Recently he had been in pain, and she was worried about him.

"Why do you not see the Doctor, Papa?" she asked.

"Because he can do nothing for me," her father replied. "The War may have ended, but French bullets linger on!"

He had laughed at his own joke, but Benita had not found it funny.

She loved her father and he was all she had.

They were very quiet in the part of the country where they lived, even though it was not many miles from London.

It was North, while it was more fashionable for people to go South.

Especially since the Prince Regent had made Brighton so important.

He had built a magnificent Pavilion that Benita longed to see.

Her father was very reticent about the Social World which she would have entered had her mother still been alive.

"You will have to wait a little while, my dearest," he said to everything she suggested.

"But now that I am eighteen, I am old enough to go to a Ball, Papa, and I would love to visit Almack's and see even people as important as the Duke of Wellington dancing."

Her father had laughed.

"The Duke was turned away from Almack's the other night because he was wearing trousers instead of knee-breeches!"

"That must have been very frustrating for him," Benita said.

"It is a good thing somebody keeps up a sense of propriety!" her father replied sharply.

Benita knew this was a sore point with him.

Not only manners and social customs had deteriorated but so had morals.

"I will not have you mixing with men who have forgotten how to behave like Gentlemen!" he had said more than once.

Benita had not argued, as she never did with her father.

At the same time, she thought she would never be able to dance if she did not meet any men.

Sometimes her father had danced with her in the past when her mother had played the piano.

Once a week she had dancing lessons with an old Professor.

It was not the same as going to a Ball.

At the same time, as long as she could ride the fine horses her father had added to the stables and be with him, she had no wish to complain.

The house came in sight and she thought how attractive it was.

Not very large, it was an Elizabethan Manor with high gables and strange twisting chimneys.

It had belonged, before her father and mother moved in, to a family who had owned it for over two hundred years.

"How could they bear to give it up" Benita had asked when they first came to the Manor.

"Drink, cards and dice!" her father replied enigmatically.

There was a scathing note in his voice which told her he did not wish to pursue the subject.

She therefore had asked her mother the same question when they were alone.

"It is a sad story," her mother said. "The people who lived here had only one son. They were the last of a very long and distinguished family."

Benita was listening attentively and her mother went on:

"Their only son, however, got caught up with the reckless young Bucks and *Beaux* who spend their time drinking and gambling."

Benita gave a little cry.

"Do you mean he gambled away the house and the estate, Mama?"

"That is exactly what he did," her mother said. "I believe that after he had done so he lost his life in a foolish duel which he fought with a man who was a far better shot than he was."

Benita thought it was a very sad story.

At the same time, she could not help being glad that she had such a beautiful home.

There was a garden, sloping down to a small stream, which came under her mother's care.

With the help of a large number of gardeners it was as beautiful, Benita thought, as the gardens at Vauxhall.

She had never been to Vauxhall Gardens, but she had heard about them, and how colourful they were.

There was an Orchestra playing, with singers from overseas.

Many of the *Beau Ton* had supper there, besides a crowd of ordinary citizens who just wanted to look.

'Perhaps one day I shall see Vauxhall Gardens,' she thought wistfully.

At the same time, she was thrilled with the smooth lawns, the rhododendrons, the azaleas and the lilacs.

They made her own garden a Paradise in the Spring.

Ahead of her she saw a carriage moving from the front-door towards the stables.

She gave her horse a little touch with the whip which made him spring forward.

A groom was waiting outside the front-door and she slipped from the saddle before he could assist her.

Then she ran up the steps and in through the front-door.

"Papa! Papa!" she called.

As she expected, she heard his voice answering her from the Library.

"Benita!"

She ran from the hall down the passage and in through the Library door.

He was already seated at his desk.

He held out his arms as she flung herself against him.

"You are home! Oh, Papa, how wonderful! I thought, as you did not come back last night, that you would not be here until late this evening."

Her father kissed her before he said:

"I am sorry about last night, my darling, but I had a great many things to see to, and when it was dark I thought it wiser to wait until this morning."

"Much, much wiser!" Benita agreed. "You know when there is ice on the roads it is dangerous to drive as quickly as you like to do."

Her father smiled.

"I am always in a hurry to get back to you, my precious."

She sat on his knee and put her arms round his neck.

"And I have been counting the hours until I could be with you, Papa."

The only resemblance between them was that they both had bright blue eyes – the gentian blue of an alpine flower.

Otherwise, with her small pointed face and fragile appearance, Benita resembled her mother.

"Your mother was the most beautiful person I have ever
seen," her father once told her. "The minute I walked
into the Ball-Room, I knew she was the girl I wanted to
marry, and that I would storm Heaven itself to make her
my wife!"

"How romantic, Papa!" Benita exclaimed.

Her father was looking at her now.

He could see with a stab in his heart how she had her
mother's hair, her mother's white skin.

Although she was completely unaware of it, her beauty
was breath-taking.

Major Richard Grenfel was a very good-looking man
himself.

Now his hair was beginning to turn grey at the temples,
and the pain he suffered from his wounds had etched deep
lines on his face.

At the same time, his features were unchanged.

His straight nose, square forehead and firm chin pro-
claimed the blue blood which flowed in his veins.

"What have you been doing, Papa?" Benita was asking
as she pressed her cheek affectionately against his.

"That is what I am going to tell you, my darling," he
said, "so let us sit down comfortably by the fire. I am
feeling the cold to-day."

Benita slipped off his knee.

At the same time she looked at him anxiously.

He would never complain to her.

Yet she knew that the pain he suffered from his wound
was invariably worse in the winter.

The cold weather also affected his chest.

His voice was deeper and more hoarse than it was in the
summer.

There was a big fire burning in the grate on the other side of the room.

A comfortable sofa had been drawn up in front of it.

Major Grenfel moved towards it slowly and sat down with a little wince.

Benita moved beside him and put her head on his shoulder.

"What are you planning, Papa?" she asked.

"How do you know I am planning anything?" her father enquired.

Benita laughed.

"You know my intuition is almost as good as yours, and as you have cultivated it ever since I was a child, you must not be surprised when I use it!"

Major Grenfel hesitated a moment before he said:

"I want you to use it now, my precious, and realise that I love you and anything I plan is because I know it is right for you."

He spoke in such a serious way that Benita looked at him in surprise.

"Of course I know that, Papa, and you know that I love you, too, and trust you."

"That is what I want you to say," her father replied, "and I want you to promise me that you will do exactly what I ask."

"You are frightening me," Benita protested. "What is it that you want me to do that makes you speak so seriously?"

Major Grenfel looked away from her towards the fire.

Then he said:

"I saw the Doctor in London last week, and he told me what I knew already – that I have not long to live!"

Benita gave a cry.

"Oh, no, Papa! Do not say that! I have prayed, prayed

that you would get better and not suffer."

"I know your prayers have helped me, darling," her father answered. "At the same time I know, because the pain is getting worse, that it is only a question of time before I have to leave you."

Benita gave a little sob and turned her face against her shoulder.

"You are not to cry, my dearest," he said. "I shall be with your mother, and although you cannot see us, we shall both be looking after you."

"I know you will do that, Papa, but it will not be the same as having you..with me and being able to..talk and..laugh with..you."

Major Grenfel shut his eyes for a moment.

His lips tightened as if he could hardly bear to listen to what Benita was saying.

Then with an effort he said:

"Because you are sensible, and as we both know, very intelligent, you will understand that knowing what I do I have to provide for you in the future."

Benita pressed herself a little closer to him.

She did not speak and Major Grenfel went on:

"It has worried me greatly for a long time what I should do about you."

He paused before he said:

"You know I have no relatives left. Those who remain of your mother's family – and I have long ago lost touch with them – live in the North of Scotland."

"I have no wish to go to Scotland, Papa!" Benita said quickly.

"I know that," her father said. "At the same time, my adorable little daughter, I have to leave you with some-body who will look after you."

Benita raised her head.

There were tears in her eyes as she looked at her father questioningly.

"What are you..saying? Oh, Papa, I do not..want to live..with a lot of..strangers."

Her father sighed.

"I realise now, my darling, that I have been very selfish in not entertaining and bringing home the sort of people you would have met if your mother had been alive."

"I would much..rather be..with you, Papa," Benita murmured.

"That is what I wanted," her father agreed. "But it was wrong of me, very wrong."

He spoke in a way which made Benita say:

"It was not wrong, Papa. It was right..and I have been so very..very happy with you. Why should we trouble ourselves with other people when we can be together?"

There was silence before her father said very slowly:

"Now you must understand that I have to find somebody to take my place."

"No..No.." Benita cried.

As she said this she wondered wildly who she could suggest, but her father went on:

"You are not only exceedingly beautiful, but you are, my dearest, a very rich young woman!"

"*Very* rich?" Benita questioned accentuating the adverb.

"Yes, and it is that which will attract the fortune-hunters," her father answered.

His voice sharpened as he added:

"They will woo you, compliment you, and entreat you to marry them."

He paused a moment and then went on:

"But all that will really interest them is your money."

His voice was harsh and bitter.

"In that case, Papa, you must not let me have so much money. Then even if I am alone, I will not be deceived by such men."

"They are very voluble and very insidious," her father replied. "They worm their way into a woman's confidence like poisonous snakes!"

Benita shivered.

Then Major Grenfel said in a different tone of voice:

"That is why, my lovely one, you have to trust me to protect you from such despicable creatures, and make sure you are out of their reach."

"How can you do that, Papa?" Benita enquired.

Her father's arms tightened around her and she knew he had difficulty in giving the answer.

Then slowly he said:

"I have arranged, my dearest, for you to – be married!"

Benita stared at him in sheer astonishment.

It had never crossed her mind that he would think of such a thing.

Because her father and mother had been so blissfully happy together, she had told herself a Fairy Story.

It was mixed up with her dreams in which she met a man, tall and handsome, like her father.

He was the 'Prince Charming' who would sweep her off her feet.

Because they loved each other they would be married and live happily ever after.

Now what her father had said was a shock, like being suddenly dowsed with cold water.

"I..I do not..understand," she murmured.

"I have chosen the man who is to be your husband," her father said, "who has the right ideas and the right sort of character."

"B.but..I have never..met him, Papa."

"I know that," her father said, "but unfortunately, there is not time for the usual preliminaries to your marriage because I shall not be here to see them taking place."

Again Benita gave a little cry and said:

"Oh, no, Papa..it cannot be true what the Doctors said..they..must be wrong..Oh, Papa..how can you leave me..I cannot live..without you."

Major Grenfel could feel her trembling against him.

He thought that no physical agony could be worse than what he was suffering now.

Then with a superhuman effort he said very quietly:

"You have never failed me in the past, and I want you now, my dearest dear, to try to understand what I am doing."

He stopped speaking to look at her before he continued:

"Believe me when I tell you that it is what I want before I die."

Benita did not answer, and he knew she was crying.

"I thought you loved me" he said, "but if this is too much to ask, I must just let things take their course. But I swear to you it will – break my heart!"

He knew as he spoke that he was making sure Benita could not refuse him.

After what seemed a long silence, in a very small voice he could hardly hear, she said:

"I..I do love you, Papa! I love you..more than..anything else in the ..whole world..and I will..do what you..want."

Major Grenfel drew in a deep breath.

He had fought a hard battle but he had won.

"Thank you, my precious," he said simply. "You are – being married..this afternoon."

Benita raised her head to look at him as if she could not

believe what she had heard.

Her cheeks were wet with tears, her eyes misty with them.

At the same time, she looked so lovely that her father could only stare at her.

He was thinking that if she was seen in London every young Waster in the Clubs of St. James's would be at her feet.

He knew only too well how plausible they could be.

They ceased to be gentle when they were chasing golden guineas to fling on the green baize tables.

Nothing mattered to their inane minds but the turn of a card or their ridiculous, often insane, bets.

He knew their compelling blandishments which any woman, whatever her age, found hard to resist.

How could Benita, innocent, unspoiled and utterly un-sophisticated, survive?

He knew only too well it would be like putting a little white dove into a nest of hawks or eagles.

'I have to save her!' he thought frantically.

He felt a sudden panic rising within him at the idea of her alone and unprotected.

He drew her closer to him again.

"Shall I tell you what I have planned?" he asked.

He spoke in the gentle voice in which he had talked to her as a child, when she was frightened about something.

"Y.yes, Papa!"

"It is," he went on, "that you should be with a man who I know will protect you from the greed, the hypocrisy and the lies of these men I have described to you."

"B.but suppose..when I meet him..I do not like..this man you have..chosen for me?"

"You will like him," her father answered. "But of course you both will have to work to make sure that what you feel for each other is not just a pleasant attraction but the Divine Love that your mother and I had for each other."

He knew Benita with her face hidden against him was listening, and he answered:

"It is the love that all men seek, and which you have read about in your books, and which we have talked about from time to time."

He paused before he said very softly:

"It is the love of Romeo and Juliet. The love you hear played in music and whispered by the wind under the trees."

Benita made a little murmur and he went on:

"It is the love that your mother expended on the garden; a love which whenever I see the flowers and the blossom makes me feel as if I am kissing her once again."

The throb in his voice was very moving, and Benita said in a whisper:

"That..is what I wanted to..find."

"And that is what you must seek, my beautiful little daughter," her father said, "and my intuition tells me that you will find it, although perhaps not at once."

"But..I have to..marry this..man you have..chosen for me..." Benita murmured.

"It is impossible for us to wait," her father said, "and therefore the wedding will take place late this afternoon."

Benita sat bolt upright.

"Do you..really mean..this afternoon?"

"Yes, this afternoon!"

As he repeated the words, he felt a sudden pain strike through him.

Major Grenfel put his hand to his heart.

His eyes closed and Benita saw the blood leave his face.

"Papa! Papa!" she cried.

"My – drops," he murmured.

She felt in the pocket of his coat and found the small bottle.

Then she ran across the room to the grog-tray in the corner.

She knew exactly how many drops to put into the glass and how much water to add.

Then she ran back to her father.

His eyes were still closed and he was lying back against the cushions.

Terrified she saw he was too weak to hold the glass himself.

She lifted his head very gently and held the glass to his lips.

He drank the medicine.

After a few seconds the colour began to creep back into his face.

He opened his eyes.

"I – am sorry – my darling," he said in a hoarse voice.

"Stay very still, Papa," Benita said. "Shall I ring for the servants to help you upstairs?"

"No – no – I am all – right," her father managed to say.

They sat in silence for some minutes until the drops did their work.

"I must go on with what I was saying," he said aloud.

"It is..better for you..to rest, Papa."

"There is no time for that," he said. "There is so much that has to be said."

Benita moved near to him again and he put his arm round her.

"As I have already told you," he began, "you will be very rich, and I know that you, of all people, will want to help those who are less fortunate."

"Yes..of course, Papa. It is what you and Mama

have..always done, even when you were..very poor..yourselves."

"We tried to do what we could," her father said, "and no one can do more."

"I will..do the..same," Benita promised.

He did not answer and after a moment she said nervously:

"Tell..tell me about my..wedding."

"I have brought a special gown with me from London," her father said, "and you will wear your mother's veil, and the tiara which she always told me was a waste of money."

There was a faint smile on his lips as he said:

"No jewels could adorn her like the sparkle of her eyes, and the sunshine on her hair! I can say the same of you, my dearest child."

"But you..want me to..wear the..tiara?"

"The wedding will be a very quiet one," her father replied, "but it is a ceremony I want you to remember in the years ahead."

Benita felt a little shiver run through her.

She knew it was the fear of being married to a man she had never seen.

She did not even know his name.

Then she told herself that the only thing she could do was to make her father happy before he died.

Any sacrifice was worthwhile.

She must save him from suffering more than he had already and put his mind at peace.

But every nerve in her body shrank from what he asked her.

How could she marry an unknown man and be alone with him?

"How can I do anything so frightening, Mama?" she

asked in her heart.

Then somehow she knew that her mother was with them.

She was close to her father as she had always been.

She had loved him so whole-heartedly that Benita often wondered if there was room for her.

"It is Papa who..matters," she said to herself.

It was not until later, when she knew her father had recovered some of his strength, that she asked:

"Where..are you..taking me..for my..wedding?"

There was a pause, and Benita said quickly:

"You *are* taking me to the Church, Papa?"

"Because I think it will be too much for me," her father answered, "and because it would spoil the Service if I was taken ill, I have arranged for Dawson to take you."

Benita thought that everything was becoming even more frightening.

How could she be married without her father beside her?

How could she meet for the first time the man her father had chosen for her at the altar?

The man who was to be her husband.

Then she told herself sensibly that it was her father's decision and he had never misled her in the past.

Why should he do so now?

At the same time she asked piteously:

"And..when I am..married..do I go..away with my..h.husband?"

"You will of course go to his house," her father explained. "It is in fact only a journey of an hour and a half from where you are being married."

Benita gripped her fingers together until they hurt.

She wanted to ask how she could go away with this stranger.

She looked at her father.

She knew that although he was better, he was still in pain, and still weak.

"I must not..upset him," she told herself.

At the same time, she wanted to scream out a dozen objections to what was planned.

To make every possible plea that her wedding should be postponed.

At least until she knew more about it than she did now.

Then, once again, she made herself think of her father and not of herself.

She knew without any Doctor telling her that his life hung by a thread.

She remembered her mother telling her over and over again how careful they had to be with him.

"It is not only his wounds," her mother said, "but it is that his heart has been affected by all he has suffered and by the War itself."

She had given a deep sigh.

"Nobody could have been as happy as we were before he left me to join his Regiment. Now I have to pay for it!"

When her father was brought home to them on a stretcher Benita realised that he and her mother were even happier than they had been before.

Even when she was desperately worried about him, her mother had been happy.

For he was with her again. She could see him and touch him.

Benita remembered when her father was overseas, how her mother spent half the night on her knees praying.

She was beseeching the Saints in Heaven to bring him home safely.

She read every report that came back to England about the suffering and casualties in Portugal.

They made her feel as if she was being pierced by a thousand swords.

Benita was sure it was her love that had restored her father's health.

It was love not the Doctor which healed his wounds.

Love which brought him to his feet far quicker than they had expected.

And it was love that made him use his brilliant brain.

It told him how they would live far more comfortably than they had done before.

There had been times when they were so poor that Benita could remember going to bed hungry.

She had not disturbed her mother.

But when everyone was asleep she groped her way down the stairs to the kitchen.

She would search for a crust of bread or an apple to stave off her hunger.

Then when her father had gone to London everything had changed.

He had come back with a determination about him.

It told her he would be successful in what he was undertaking.

She did not, however, know what it was.

There were a few months when he went to London every day and came back late in the evening.

Then everything began to change.

First there was good food, servants and new horses.

Then they moved into The Manor which her mother had said was the house of her dreams.

It had all been wonderful.

Only when her mother had died unexpectedly one very cold winter was there a dark cloud over their happiness.

It took a long time to disperse.

Benita had her father, and her father had her.

She had the idea, although he did not say so, that they grew richer and richer.

She wanted for nothing.

She had Tutors, Governesses, Music-Teachers who were more experienced than those who had taught her previously.

They trebled in number.

Then when she was eighteen, she required them no longer.

It was then, to her unmistakable joy, that her father spent more time with her.

She knew, although he did not say so, it was because there was no longer the urgency for him to work so hard.

They had as much money as they could possibly need.

The horses in the stables were certainly the best it was possible to imagine.

Gowns filled her wardrobe.

Benita thought they would have graced the ladies who went to Carlton House or Buckingham Palace.

"Everything is wonderful!" she had told herself only that morning when she rose to go riding.

Then this bomb-shell, this explosion!

It was so overwhelming that she could not think clearly.

Her father was sitting staring into the fire.

Because she was so closely attuned to him, she knew that he was forcing himself not to worry.

He was convinced that everything he had planned was best for her.

It would give her all he wanted her to have.

Benita knelt down on the floor beside him.

She looked up at him, then she said:

"I love you..Papa! And I will do..exactly what you..want me to. At the..same time..I need your..help and..your guidance."

Her hand was resting on her father's knee and now his own covered it.

"Wherever I am, and I only hope that God will be kind enough to let me into Heaven," he said, "I shall be looking after you, and be near you if you need me."

"I shall always need you, Papa, as I need you now.'

His fingers tightened on hers, but he did not speak.

Then in a voice he could hardly hear and which shook as she spoke, Benita asked:

"What is the..name of the..man I..I am to marry?"

"His name," her father said slowly, "is the Earl of Inchester."

CHAPTER THREE

The Earl left Rustuss Groon's dingy office and walked slowly back towards Piccadilly.

He felt as if he could not think clearly and that his legs were unsteady.

How was it possible?

How could it happen that he had promised to marry the daughter of a hated Usurer?

Rustuss Groon was sinister in a way it was hard to describe.

The Earl was well aware that he was astute.

Nothing missed the eyes that were veiled by his dark glasses.

The Earl could see his long black hair falling over the sides of his face and his hunched figure.

He was terrified when he thought of what his daughter would be like.

"How can I have agreed? Was there no other way?"

The questions seemed to repeat and repeat themselves with the sound his footsteps made on the dirty pavement.

Then he was moving through the traffic of Piccadilly

back towards St. James's Street.

He told Sir Anthony that he would go home.

Now he knew he did not want to be alone.

"Has this really happened?" he asked himself. "Or have I just dreamt it?"

He had not however dreamt the money that lay heavy in his pocket.

Only Rustuss Groon, he thought, would have given it to him in sovereigns.

"I am sure" the Usurer had said before he left, "that you will require some money before the wedding takes place."

He had opened a drawer of his desk.

He took out a bag which clinked as he put it on the desk and said:

"Here are thirty sovereigns."

He had already explained briefly the Earl was to be married in a Private Chapel the very next afternoon.

There were still several Private Chapels in the country.

They did not require the formalities of a Special Licence, as was usual in other Churches.

Yet the Chaplain was empowered to marry whomsoever he chose, and at any time he was required to do so.

The Private Chapel to which the Earl was to go had belonged to Lord Bradford who had fled the country.

The Earl remembered Sir Anthony Keswick had said Lord Bradford had borrowed money from Rustuss Groon. He was a man he had never liked.

But if the Usurers would no longer lend him money, it was a choice of Prison or exile.

The Earl had accepted the sovereigns without finding anything to say, and the hoarse voice continued:

"Once you are married, a carriage will be waiting for you outside the Chapel, and from there you will drive to

Inch Hall."

He paused before he said as if he had suddenly thought of it:

"You rode into London on a horse, but you certainly cannot ride back in your wedding-garments. I will therefore arrange that a Travelling Chariot will pick you up from wherever you are staying."

The Earl, who had intended to return home that evening, knew from the way Rustuss Groon spoke that he would be expected to appear in better clothing than he was wearing at the moment.

When he thought of what remained of his clothes at home, he knew they were in even worse repair than what he had on.

The only answer was to borrow from Sir Anthony.

He therefore said in a grim voice because he was angry at being manipulated:

"I am staying at 95 Half Moon Street."

"Very well," Rustuss Groon answered. "The Travelling Chariot will be outside at a quarter to three tomorrow afternoon. It will not take more than an hour with two horses to reach the Chapel. Your horse will be taken back to Inch Hall."

As the Earl walked on he was thinking that only a Sorcerer or a Wizard could know so much.

How could Rustuss Groon have been aware how he had come to London.

Or know that he had nothing respectable to wear.

"The man is not human!" he decided.

He felt the bag of gold heavy in his pocket.

It was appropriate, he thought bitterly, that he had been given thirty sovereigns.

They should actually have been pieces of silver.

He had sold himself, his freedom and his pride as Judas

had sold his Master.

He walked into White's Club and was greeted respectfully by the porter.

To his relief he saw that Sir Anthony was still there.

He gave an exclamation of delight when the Earl walked towards him.

As he reached him he said:

"You have come back, Garth! I hoped you would! What happened?"

"Let me get my breath back," the Earl said as he sat down.

Sir Anthony took one look at him and said:

"He has refused you!"

The Earl shook his head.

"No, he agreed."

"Then why are you looking so 'down in the mouth'?" his friend asked.

Suddenly the Earl decided he could not tell his friend Anthony or anybody else what he had agreed to do.

He knew only too well the expression of horror he would see on Anthony's face.

It would be difficult to explain that what he was doing was not for himself.

It was to save those who depended on him.

Yet he knew that practically every man in the room would think him a fool.

He would be marrying not only out of his class but also the daughter of a man they hated.

While they were forced to be obliged to Rustuss Groon, at the same time they hated or despised him.

Having made up his mind that he would keep his secret, the Earl said:

"The gruesome Groon has met my demands."

"Well, thank God for that!" Sir Anthony exclaimed.

"And I am glad you have come back to celebrate."

As he spoke he signalled to a steward to hurry with another bottle of champagne.

"I will pay for this one," the Earl said.

"You will do nothing of the sort!" Sir Anthony replied. "Whatever you have managed to squeeze out of Groon you will pay for with hard work, as well as the amount of cash you will have to return to him sooner or later."

The Earl did not reply.

He was thinking he would not pay in cash, but in years of shame and humiliation.

He would have a wife he would be ashamed to present to his friends.

A wife he would hide away rather than have to explain who was her father.

He would only have to mention the name 'Groon' and they would know exactly what had happened.

He could imagine only too well the contemptuous manner in which they would speak of him in the Clubs.

He could hear the scathing remarks they would make about his wife, as well as any children they produced.

Unless he was careful, there would be cartoons depicting him weighing the woman who bore his name.

She would be as wide as a pair of scales balanced against a pile of golden sovereigns like those he carried in his pocket.

"How can I do it? How can I drag the name of which my ancestors have been so proud not through the dust, but a sewer?"

Sir Anthony was handing him a glass of champagne.

"Cheer up!" he said. "You have got what you wanted, and although inevitably there will be a 'day of reckoning' it may not come for several years."

"On the contrary," the Earl wanted to say, "it comes

to-morrow!"

He drank the champagne.

After several glasses he felt that his brain had not cleared but was becoming so bemused that he could not think at all.

Then, though the voice seemed far away, he heard Sir Anthony ask:

"When did you last have something to eat?"

"I cannot remember," the Earl answered. "I think it was at breakfast."

"Then we will have something to eat now," Sir Anthony said, "and I will stand you a dinner the equal of what you would have at Carlton House."

He ordered pâté sandwiches.

The Earl consumed several and felt a little better.

They finished the champagne.

Then Sir Anthony suggested taking the Earl back to his flat in Half Moon Street to change.

"Fortunately we are about the same size," he said, "although you are thinner than me round the waist, doubtless because you work harder!"

He laughed before he added:

"Or shall I say you work on the soil while I take my exercise in bed!"

The Earl knew that Sir Anthony was boasting about his amatory prowess.

But he was an excellent rider and an accomplished swordsman.

They drove in Sir Anthony's Phaeton, which he had left outside the Club, to Half Moon Street.

He had a large flat.

It had a comfortable extra bedroom in which he could accommodate a guest if he wished to do so.

Now he told his Valet to prepare a bath for the Earl.

Also, he added, to provide His Lordship with some evening-clothes.

The Earl would not have been human if he had not appreciated the bath that was prepared for him in front of a roaring fire.

He soaked away the grime of his journey to London.

Also his anger cooled and a resentment which made him feel that instead of a heart he had a stone in his chest.

After his bath he was arrayed in a high cravat and a smart tail-coat that belonged to Sir Anthony.

With this he wore a pair of long black drainpipe pantaloons which had been invented by the Prince Regent.

He began to feel like a different man.

"My last night of freedom," he said to his reflection in the mirror.

As he did so he swore once again that when he returned to the country no one should see his wife.

That meant that he too must exile himself from his friends.

When he went into the Sitting-Room it was to find that Sir Anthony was as smartly dressed as he was.

He forced a smile.

"This is like old times, Tony, for us to be going out together, wondering what we shall find."

"I can answer that only too easily," Sir Anthony replied, "but it rather depends on you."

"I am in your hands."

"Then that is a different matter altogether ," his friend laughed.

He took him first to the Thatched House Tavern where the food was reputed to be outstanding.

"As good," Sir Anthony said, "as what is provided by the Prince Regent's Chef at Carlton House."

The Earl thought as course succeeded course that only a

French Chef could have created what he and Anthony were eating.

They were offered different wines.

Maderia, Hock, Champagne, Hermitage, Burgundy, Bordeaux and Port.

It was with the greatest difficulty that the Earl refused several of these, much to the disappointment of the wine waiter.

Instead of Port he asked for a small glass of brandy.

They then went on to the White House, which the Earl had visited in the past.

He thought a little cynically that it had not changed.

Except that many of the patrons had grown older and *Madame's* voice was shriller.

There were the same gambling-tables in the centre of the room.

The same loud calls of the *Croupier*.

The same voices rising in excitement as somebody won.

The same groan of despair when another fool lost.

Standing beside those at the gaming-tables were the most expensive prostitutes in London.

They were described by many names.

'Cyprians', 'Nuns', 'Soiled Doves', 'Aspasias', 'Vestals', all meaning the same thing.

In their appearance, their conversation and their greed for money they were almost indistinguishable from one another.

At the sight of the Earl and Sir Anthony there were screeches of delight.

Several of those who were not already engaged ran towards them.

They hung on the men's arms, looking up at them invitingly and pouting their lips provocatively.

After a few words of greeting one of them was whispering enticingly in the Earl's ear.

He shook his head.

Sir Arthur ordered drinks for two of the more alluring of them.

After they had laughed and talked Sir Anthony, in a voice only the Earl could hear, asked:

"Do you feel like taking either of these upstairs?"

"I do not!" the Earl said firmly.

"Very well, let us move on."

Sir Anthony gave the Cyprians a few sovereigns and he and the Earl drove off again in the carriage.

"Where shall we go?" Sir Anthony enquired.

"I have no idea," the Earl replied. "This is your party."

"Very well," Sir Anthony said. "We will go to the Wolves' Club."

The Earl raised his eye-brows.

"This is new, at any rate."

"You will enjoy it," Sir Anthony went on. "The members are composed almost wholly of people connected with the Theatre."

He went on to say that their Club met in the Harp Tavern, a well-known Theatrical House, just by Drury Lane Theatre.

There was dramatic entertainment, two outstanding singers, amusing 'turns,' dirty jokes, and a great number of attractive women.

There were actresses, 'Bits o' Muslin', and what were known as Buttocks or Bulks.

There were the women who worked with the bullyboy thieves.

They managed by some means of their own to get into every Club or Tavern.

It was certainly amusing, and the Earl was not surprised to see members of White's and Boodles there.

There were also the obsessed gamblers, who took no notice of the entertainment, but continued to play cards amongst themselves.

From there they wandered on to The Coal Hole, which was kept by Rhodes, the Singing Collier.

Edmund Kean, the brilliant actor, had been a nightly visitor until he had founded the Wolves' Club.

Although he was a genius on the stage, he was a very strange character off it.

They did not find him at either place tonight.

Sir Anthony learnt that after the Theatre he had been in The Coal Hole for a short while, then left.

"God knows what he is doing," Sir Anthony said. "He will often take his favourite horse and ride madly through the night across London and out into the country."

"Why does he do that?" the Earl asked.

"He jumps the toll-gates in Highwayman fashion, yells at the turnpike-keepers, then comes back in the early morning to his house in Clarges Street, covered in dust, and half dead."

The Earl thought it must be a relief from some arduous role he was playing.

He wondered if the day would come when he would do something similar.

It would be a relief from his hideous wife and his dependence on her money.

"You are looking gloomy again," Sir Anthony said. "Where else shall I take you?"

"Nowhere," the Earl replied, "let us go back and go to bed."

"It is only three o'clock," Sir Anthony said. "What about dropping into White's and playing a few hands at the card-tables, or, if you prefer, we could go to Wattier's?"

"I prefer neither," the Earl replied.

He had left the thirty sovereigns which Rustuss Groon had given him in a locked drawer in the flat.

He had no intention of spending any of it in London.

Every penny was to be used in helping his pensioners.

They were his most pressing concern, and after them would come thousands of other things.

He did not feel embarrassed at sponging on Sir Anthony for food this evening because he was very rich.

He knew his offer of help had been perfectly sincere when he had offered him a 'monkey'.

Five hundred pounds would not have mattered to him one way or another.

The Earl knew only too well how some young men sponged on their rich friends.

He had sworn years ago it was something he would never do himself.

They drove back to the flat in Half Moon Street and the Earl said:

"Thank you, Tony. I have enjoyed this evening, and it is something I shall remember."

"For God's sake, Garth, you are young and healthy!" his friend replied. "Do not bury yourself in the country."

He paused a moment and then went on:

"There are other things in the world besides your house, your crops and those tiresome pensioners who worry you so much."

"I am sure there are," the Earl agreed. "At the same time, I have to be responsible for them."

" 'Any man with an obsession is a bore'!" Sir Anthony quipped.

The Earl laughed.

"Then that is what I have been for a long time."

Sir Anthony put his hand on his friend's shoulder.

"You know I am only joking, Garth! There is no one more amusing or more interesting and at the same time as dedicated as you are."

He paused before he added:

"But you are still young. You should enjoy yourself. You'll be a long time dead!"

"You are trying to tempt me," the Earl laughed, "and I can only say 'Get thee behind me, Satan!' and go on being a bore!"

"Then I only hope you enjoy your harp!" Sir Anthony said with a sigh. "You will certainly have a front seat in Heaven, but I have often thought myself that 'twanging a harp round a sapphire sea' would inevitably pall after the first few hours!"

The Earl laughed.

"I will not forget to send a few drops of water to wherever you are. If it is as hot as the Preachers predict it will be, you will need them."

"I have a feeling I will be in the company of a large number of friends who will find their throats are dry from the heat of the flames!"

They were both laughing as they went to their separate bedrooms.

The Earl got into bed.

He told himself that if Tony had been aware that this was his last night of bachelorhood, he could not have tried harder to keep him amused.

"Perhaps if I did not have so many worries, and one particular one," he thought, "I should have enjoyed it more."

He had listened to the songs, applauded the acts and laughed at the jokes.

He had also heard the voice of a 'Cyprian' whispering of untold delights.

Yet behind it all he could see Rustuss Groon.

If his daughter resembled him, then the sooner he too wore dark glasses the better.

He did not expect to sleep.

But he had lain awake most of the previous night.

He was asking himself how in Heaven he should be-seech Rustuss Groon to be generous.

Now he had won, but at what cost?

He was too tired to think about it and fell into a dream-less slumber.

The Earl awoke horrified to find that it was eleven o'clock.

He opened the door and called Sir Anthony's Valet who quickly appeared.

"Why did you not wake me?" the Earl asked.

"Oi 'ears wot time Yer Lordship an' the Master comes in las' night," the Valet replied, "an' Oi thinks p'raps a little 'shut-eye' would do ye both good."

He pulled back the curtains as he added:

"If ye get back into bed, M'Lord, Oi'll 'ave yer break-fast ready in a few minutes."

"Is Sir Anthony still asleep?" the Earl enquired.

" 'E is, Sir, an' if Oi wakes 'im, 'e'll be in a nasty temper, an' that's for sure!"

The Earl laughed as the Valet hurried away towards the kitchen.

He knew the man had been with Sir Anthony for many years.

While he was outspoken, he looked after him like a Nanny.

His clothes were washed, pressed and mended.

He prevented him from being crooked by the trades-men he patronised in Shepherd's Market.

The Earl had eaten his breakfast and was reading the morning newspaper when Sir Anthony walked into the room yawning.

"Did you sleep well?" he asked.

"Surprisingly well," the Earl answered.

"I feel awful!" Sir Anthony remarked.

"I told you not to drink so much at dinner, although the wines were excellent."

"I know," Sir Anthony groaned, "but as I have told you before, Garth, one has to pay for everything in this life."

His words, spoken jokingly, brought back into the Earl's mind the price he was paying.

A feeling of horror swept over him like a dark cloud.

He thought for a moment that he would, after all, tell his friend his secret and his apprehension about the future.

Then he knew this was something he could confide to no one.

Even if he did, there would be no solution.

Sir Anthony told his Valet to bring him his breakfast in the Earl's room.

The man set it on a small table beside the bed, and Sir Anthony sat on the mattress and ate slowly, pouring out a cup of black coffee.

"Now I feel better!" he announced.

"If you drink like that every night," the Earl remarked, "you will die young."

"Of course," Sir Anthony replied, "but think how much I shall enjoy the years I do live!"

He gave a laugh before he went on:

"While you, my dear Garth, are being so abstemious it will only prolong the agony."

"There is many a true word spoken in jest," the Earl thought.

Perhaps when he had expended the money he needed
for everything else, he would fill the cellars at Inch Hall.

Then he could avoid the horror of looking at his wife at
the end of the table by drinking himself insensible.

This was a passing thought.

He looked at the clock and remembered he only had a
few more hours of freedom.

"There is no hurry for you to return to the country,"
Sir Anthony was saying, "and we will go and have
luncheon before you leave."

Before the Earl could reply the Valet came into the
room.

"There be two Tailors from Weston's, M'Lord, t' see
ye."

"From Weston's!" the Earl exclaimed.

He remembered as he spoke that Weston had for the
last few years been the favourite Tailor of the Prince
Regent.

He was therefore patronised by all the smartest *Beaux*
in St. James's.

"Did they actually ask for His Lordship by name?" Sir
Anthony questioned. "The coat I ordered should be ready
by now."

" 'Im distinctly says 'Th' Earl O' Inchester', unless me
ears be deceivin' me!" the Valet replied.

"Then you had better show them in!" Sir Anthony
remarked.

The two men came into the room, each carrying a large
box.

They bowed politely to both the Earl and Sir Anthony.

"What is this all about?" Sir Anthony asked.

"We were instructed, Sir, to deliver these clothes to the
Earl of Inchester," one of the men replied.

"I am he!" the Earl said.

The man bowed ever lower and said:

"These clothes, M'Lord, were ordered a week ago with instructions to have them ready by noon today."

The Earl stared at him.

"They are already paid for, M'Lord, but it would be extremely gracious if Your Lordship would try them on so that we can make any adjustments necessary."

The Earl's eyes darkened.

It was incredible, but he knew he was not mistaken!

Rustuss Groon had decided a week ago, before he wrote to him, that he should marry his daughter.

The boxes the Tailors were carrying would contain the appropriate clothes in which he would be married.

He felt his anger rising inside him.

How dare the Usurer presume that he would accept his outrageous suggestion before it was even put to him?

Then he knew it would be a mistake to show his anger in front of Sir Anthony.

The Tailors would undoubtedly talk.

He got out of bed.

There was no doubt when he dressed that the garments were in impeccable taste.

They were exactly his measurements and fitted without a wrinkel.

"Who can have given you clothes like these?" Sir Anthony asked.

"I have not the slightest idea!" the Earl replied sharply.

Feeling his friend would think it strange, he added rather lamely:

"I think it must be one of my relations who called unexpectedly and saw me looking like a scarecrow!"

"Then you must certainly express your gratitude," Sir Anthony exclaimed.

Without waiting for the Earl to reply he said to the

Tailors:

"Who ordered these things for His Lordship?"

The Earl held his breath.

If they said it was Rustuss Groon he felt that all would be up.

He would have to tell Sir Anthony the truth.

"It seems strange, Sir," one of the men replied, "but while we received explicit instructions as to measurements and the money to pay for these garments and others, there was no name attached to the order."

The Earl breathed again.

"It is certainly a surprise present," he said lightly. "I am sure I shall find out sooner or later who has given it to me."

"You certainly look better than you did yesterday!" Sir Anthony remarked.

The Earl thanked the Tailors who, bowing politely, left the room.

He looked at himself in the mirror.

The irony was that he looked exactly like a Bridegroom and at the same time a gentleman.

Rustuss Groon's taste was obviously better than his appearance.

He only hoped that he might be able to say the same thing of his daughter.

"Now you are dressed," Sir Anthony said, "I will do the same and we might as well go to White's and let them see the transformation that has taken place overnight."

"Did I really look so disreputable?" the Earl asked.

"If you want me to be frank I will tell you it was ghastly!" Sir Anthony answered. "But perhaps they thought it was an aristocratic pose like Norfolk's."

He laughed before he finished:

"He never washes or changes his linen until he is so

drunk that the servants do it when he is no longer able to protest!"

"If I looked as bad as that," the Earl said, "I would shoot myself!"

"Nonsense!" Sir Anthony retorted. "You would merely do what he does and pick up another bottle!"

The Earl laughed and threw a pillow at him.

Sir Anthony deftly avoided it and went to his own bedroom.

The Earl walked into the Sitting-Room.

It was after midday.

He had just a few more hours before the Travelling Chariot arrived to take him to the Chapel.

He thought there was little difference from going to the Old Bailey to be sentenced to death.

There he would be imprisoned until he could pay his debts – which would be never.

He caught a glimpse of himself in a long mirror.

He was not conceited.

But dressed as he was now, he knew any woman would be proud to have him as her husband.

How could he go through life hiding away his wife?

Apologising if anybody saw her, keeping her identity a secret from his closest friends?

'It is impossible!' he thought despairingly.

He looked up at the portrait of Sir Anthony's mother, who had been very beautiful.

Although he was not aware of it, he was praying.

"Do not let her be too hideous, too revolting!" he was saying beneath his breath.

The words seemed to come not from his mind but from his heart.

He knew they were not just expressions of fear, but of sheer anguish.

After an excellent luncheon at White's the Earl rose from the table.

He and Sir Anthony had been joined by several of their friends.

"How are you, Inchester?" they had all asked the Earl. "Nice to see you again."

They had noticed the clothes he was wearing.

One of them, more outspoken than the rest, remarked:

"You are looking dashed smart! Are you going to Carlton House?"

"Why should you think I am going there?" the Earl enquired.

"I thought it would upset 'Prinny' to see somebody with a good figure in the sort of clothes he wears himself!"

The speaker laughed before he continued:

"He has an excellent taste when it comes to antiques, but he has the same greedy taste in the culinary achievements of his Chefs!"

They had all laughed, and Sir Anthony said mockingly:

"That is a warning to you, Garth, not to eat what you grow!"

The Earl replied with a twinkle in his eyes:

"I will of course, take your advice, and I only hope you take mine when it comes to the third or fourth bottle!"

As his friends were still finishing their port, brandy and coffee, the Earl rose.

"I have to go," he said to Sir Anthony. "Thank you a thousand times for letting me stay with you. I have enjoyed myself enormously!"

"So have I," Sir Anthony agreed, "and do not let it be too long before we 'do the town' again."

"I shall certainly think about it," the Earl promised.

Sir Anthony saw no point in accompanying his friend.

He therefore sat down again at the table and the Earl,

with a sense of relief, left the Club.

He walked, because he felt he needed the exercise, to Half Moon Street.

When he reached it he saw a very impressive *Pilentom* Travelling coach outside Anthony's door.

As he drew nearer he appreciated the exceptionally well-bred horses that were drawing it.

As he reached the Chariot, the coachman and the groom touched their caps and the Earl said:

"I think you are waiting for me. I am the Earl of Inchester."

"Yes, M'Lord," the footman who was standing on the ground replied. "Us were told t' be 'ere at quarter-t'three."

"You are punctual!" the Earl observed.

As he spoke he realised that Sir Anthony's Valet was standing at the open door of the house.

He walked towards him.

"Oi wondered, M'Lord," the Valet said in a low voice so that he would not be overheard by the other servants, "if ye wanted th' clothes ye was wearin' yesterday, or if Oi should throw 'em away."

"I will take them with me," the Earl replied.

"Oi thinks that's wot ye'd say, Sir, an' Oi've got them packed ready for ye."

The Earl thanked him and gave him two of the gold sovereigns he had received from Rustuss Groon.

It was the first time he had taken anything out of the bag.

The Earl got into the coach.

The footman placed a fur rug over his knees.

Then he said before he shut the door:

"There be a note for Yer Lordship."

He indicated where it lay on the back-seat.

The Earl picked it up, opened the envelope and read:

"*The coach in which you are travelling is now yours and so are the servants.*"

There was no signature.

"I have to be grateful," he told himself.

Then he remembered the reason for such generosity.

It was a woman to whom he would have to express his thanks for the clothes he was wearing and the coach in which he was driving.

Also for every penny he spent.

Suppose she was a skinflint as he had been told her father was?

Suppose he had to go down on his knees and plead with her for what he expended on anything other than herself?

Admittedly by law anything a wife possessed belonged on marriage to her husband.

But he could imagine the agony of being beholden to her if she begrudged everything he spent!

"How can I endure it?" he asked himself.

The coach was already moving out of London and the horses had increased their pace.

He thought they were carrying him swiftly – far too swiftly – towards a living Hell.

CHAPTER FOUR

By the time she had dressed Benita felt panic-stricken.

She had, for the last hour or so after her father had told her what was happening, felt numb.

It was as if she could not fully comprehend what was taking place.

Then as she went upstairs she had contemplated for a moment running to the stables.

She could jump on her favourite horse *Swallow* and disappear so that no one would find her.

Her Bridegroom could wait and she would not turn up.

Her father would be angry.

Yet perhaps he would realise he must make other plans for the future.

Then she knew she could not let him down, could not make him unhapy.

He begged her to trust him and that was what she had to do.

The gown he had brought her from London was very beautiful.

It was white and glittered with tiny diamanté on the

skirt and round the neck.

There were ribbons that crossed over her breasts and cascaded down her back which were of silver.

They also were embroidered with diamanté.

The housemaid placed the veil on her hair.

She had looked after her since her Nanny, who had been with her since she was a baby, had retired.

The maid then added the tiara.

Benita was glad the veil coverd her face.

She thought her Bridegroom would not know she was hating him.

She had never heard his name before to-day.

She had no idea if he was young, old, handsome or deformed.

"Trust your father!"

She could almost hear her mother saying the words and thought she was being very ungrateful.

Her father had done so much for her and made her so happy.

How could she think of herself and not of him?

"You looks lovely, Miss Benita, an' that's th'truth!" the maid exclaimed.

"Y . you have . . packed my things?" Benita asked in a low voice.

"Yes, Miss, all your gowns, an' everything that goes with them."

"Did you remember to include the miniatures of my mother and father?"

"Of course, Miss. I knows you take 'em with you wher-ever you goes."

"Thank you, Emily."

Benita took a last look at herself in the mirror.

She thought with the veil over her face it would be difficult for anyone to see exactly what she looked like.

She threw it back so that she could kiss her father good-bye.

Downstairs she found him, as she expected, lying on the sofa in the Library.

She came towards him and he exclaimed:

"Exactly how I want you to look! You make a very beautiful Bride, my precious daughter!"

Benita moved to the sofa and went down on her knees beside him.

"You . . will be . . thinking of me, Papa, and . . praying for me?"

"You know I will," her father answered. "And as soon as it is possible persuade your husband to bring you over to see me, if . . "

He stopped.

Benita knew he was going to say "if I am still alive."

She gave a little sob.

"Oh, Papa . . darling . . wonderful Papa . . how can I go away . . like this?"

"Because it is making me very happy."

He saw the tears beginning to run down her cheeks and said:

"I shall lie here thinking about you and praying for you, and you will be aware of it all through the Marriage Service."

Benita wanted to say that it would be so different if he was beside her.

Then she was aware how pale and drawn he looked.

She knew he was in fact very ill.

"I will come to see you as soon as I possibly can," she said. "Nothing . . Papa, will keep me . . from you!"

Her voice broke on the last words.

She pressed her cheek against his so that he would not see her tears.

He held her very closely in his arms.

Then he said gently:

"Go now, my darling, and may God be with you."

Benita kissed him on both cheeks.

Because she knew it was what he wanted, she then rose from her knees.

As she walked towards the door she drew her veil back over her face.

She turned to wave her hand in a last farewell.

She wanted to speak, but it was impossible for her to do so.

She left the Library, closing the door behind her, and walked down the passage to the hall.

Waiting for her there was a man she had met only once before.

She knew that he worked with her father in London and that his name was Captain Dawson.

When she reached him he bowed and she held out her hand.

It was impossible for her to speak.

As if he understood he took her hand and slipped it through his arm.

Then he led her down the steps to where a large and comfortable closed carriage was waiting.

He helped her into it and a footman placed a fur rug over her knees.

Captain Dawson sat beside her, and the footman called out as he shut the carriage-door:

"Good Luck, Miss Benita!"

Benita could not answer.

The tears were streaming down her cheeks and she lifted her handkerchief under her veil.

The horses moved off and Captain Dawson looked out of the window.

He understood how Benita was feeling.

He knew there were no words with which he could comfort her.

They drove for a long time before Benita said in a very small voice:

"I . . I am s . sorry."

"It is all right," Captain Dawson assured her. "I understand how much it means leaving your father, but he is a very sick man."

"I . . I . . know . . that."

"Everything he has done," Captain Dawson said, "and all he has worked for, had been for your mother and for you."

"I love him . . so much," Benita said in a voice he could hardly hear. "H . how can I leave him?"

Captain Dawson did not reply.

He knew, as no one else did, how desperate the Major had been to ensure that his daughter was looked after when he was dead.

He knew of the curious, twisted, plan he had made for her protection.

He had been sworn to secrecy so that not only Benita but also the Earl would not learn of it.

"Why?" he had asked.

The reply had been:

"That is what I wish until the moment when you know it is advisable to tell them the truth."

"It is a great responsibility," Captain Dawson said to himself now.

He thought if Benita did know the truth, it might make things worse than they were already.

The horses drove on, and only when they were nearing the Private Chapel did Captain Dawson say:

"We shall be arriving in five minutes. Would you like to

borrow my handkerchief?''

He thought her own must be sodden with tears.

He knew he was right when her hand came from under her veil to take the one he offered her.

Benita wiped her eyes and told herself she must have more self-control.

At the same time, she had a strong premonition that she would never see her father again.

"If he were dead, I would not need to . . marry this terrible man who is . . waiting for me," she thought.

Then she remembered what her father had said.

She must live up to his expectations, wherever he might be.

"Thank . . you," she said in a nervous little voice to Captain Dawson.

She handed him back his handkerchief.

She was hoping frantically that her veil would hide her tear-stained face.

The horses drove in at some imposing-looking gates and there was a drive in front of them.

A second or two later they branched off onto a narrow lane which led off the drive.

They were travelling under the trees.

The Chapel was a very beautiful building.

It had been erected at the same time as the house, approximately two hundred years ago.

The trees that had been planted when it was first built had grown up to surround it.

The Earl, who had arrived earlier, thought the Chapel was very dark.

He realised it was because the stained-glass windows hardly admitted any light.

In fact the only light in the Chapel came from six candles on the altar.

The inside was not, as he had expected, dilapidated.

It had obviously been quite recently repaired and renovated.

There was a profusion of white flowers on the altar and on each side of it.

There were also flowers on the window-sills.

Their fragrance scented the air.

The Earl saw that kneeling in front of the altar which was covered with a white cloth embroidered in gold there was a Clergyman.

There was no one else in the Chapel.

He walked slowly up the carpeted aisle to take the front pew on the right-hand side.

He saw that it was carved with the coat-of-arms of the Bradford family.

He wondered who in the owner's absence could have refurbished the Chapel.

There were new red velvet cushions on the seats.

He saw too that the two cushions which had been placed in front of the altar were of white satin with gold tassels.

He had been there only a few minutes, while the Parson was still at his prayers, when he heard the sound of wheels.

He realised that with almost perfect timing his Bride had arrived.

It was then the tension within him was strained almost to breaking-point.

He knew, although he mocked at himself, that he was afraid.

Afraid of what she would be like.

Afraid of what he would see as she came towards him on her father's arm.

He moved into the aisle and stood waiting.

The Parson also rose and turned round with his back to

the altar.

He was an elderly man with a saintly face and white hair.

The Earl, however, was looking at the two figures coming in through the West Door.

He saw at once that the man was not Rustuss Groon.

But he recognised him as the man who had been with Groon in his office each time he had been there.

Now he looked very different from how he had appeared on those occasions.

He was as smartly dressed as he was himself.

Although he was older, he carried himself, the Earl thought, as upright as if he had been a soldier.

Then when his eyes would have moved to the Bride, he found he could not bring himself to look at her.

He turned away and only when she stood beside him was he acutely conscious of her presence.

At the same time, he looked straight ahead at the Parson.

Without any preliminaries the Service began.

The Parson spoke with a quiet sincerity which made it impossible not to feel the sanctity of what was taking place.

He asked:

"Who giveth this woman to be married to this man?"

Captain Dawson replied in a quiet voice:

"I do."

He turned to the Earl.

As he made his responses, his voice sounded to him hard and almost too loud.

He was fighting for self-control.

In contrast Benita's voice was hardly audible and little above a whisper.

It was then the Earl realised in dismay that he had not

thought of a ring.

He had shied away from contemplating the Service which lay ahead of him.

He had therefore never considered that he had something to contribute towards the Service.

To his relief Captain Dawson drew a ring from his pocket and handed it to him.

It was, Benita realised, as the Earl put it on her finger, her mother's ring.

She realised her father had sent it deliberately.

It was symbolic of the love he wanted her to have.

It fitted her perfectly.

Now for the first time since she had entered the Chapel she felt that her mother was near her.

She could see her face clearly.

The softness of the love in her eyes, the smile on her lips.

"Help me . . Mama . . help . . me!" she cried in her heart.

As if it was an answer she remembered that the ring encircling her finger had never been removed from her mother's hand until she died.

It symbolised seventeen years of blissful happiness.

"Mama . . is . . with me," Benita thought as she and the Earl knelt for the final blessing.

When they rose to their feet the Parson pointed with his hand to a small table just below the altar steps.

On it was the Marriage Register, an ink-pot and two quill pens.

The Earl picked one up and signed his name where the Parson directed.

It was difficult to see as the light from the altar did not reach the table.

As he put down the quill pen Benita took the other to

sign her name beneath his.

Then for the first time since they had entered the Chapel there was the sound of an organ.

It was playing softly, and was out of sight.

Without speaking either to the Parson or to Captain Dawson, the Earl offered Benita his arm.

They walked down the aisle to music which seemed to fill the small building with a paean of praise to God.

They reached the door and outside there was waiting a carriage.

It was not that in which either the Earl or Benita had arrived.

It was a Britchka chariot which had been invented only a few years before.

It was used by those who wished to travel very swiftly and comfortably.

There was no coachman, which meant the Earl would drive.

There was a seat for the groom behind the raised hood which covered the front seat.

It could be opened if required.

There were two fine horses to draw it.

He got into the driving-seat.

He could not repress a little feeling of excitement at the idea of controlling such magnificent horse-flesh.

He was hardly aware as he picked up the reins that Benita had been wrapped in a fur cloak.

It enveloped her from her neck to her feet.

She was helped into the seat beside him and a sable rug was placed over her knees.

There was a foot-warmer under her feet.

Captain Dawson tucked her in.

"You will be warm enough," he said. "It will only take an hour."

It was what her father had told her.

In a voice that only he could hear she said:

"You will . . look after . . Papa and . . tell him . . I love . . him?"

"You know I will do that," Captain Dawson replied. "I will tell him too that he has a very brave daughter, and he will be proud of you."

She had not raised her head and he realised that her eyes were filled with tears.

"God bless you!" he said and stood back.

The Earl moved the horses forward.

Then as they passed through the drive-gates he settled down to drive fast.

The horses were fresh and must have spent the night at a nearby stable.

Showing their paces, they went more swiftly than he had ever driven before.

He thought, although it seemed impossible, that Rustuss Groon must have a sensitive streak in him somewhere.

He must have realised that he would have no wish to talk to his Bride and she would not wish to talk to him.

They had driven quite a long way before he even glanced at her.

He could just see her tiara under the fur hood which covered her head.

It struck him, because there was so much fur, that she was like a small bear.

He wondered once again with a streak of horror if that was an animal she would resemble.

The road that led to Inch Hall, which he knew well, was a good one.

Although it could be thick with mud if the weather was wet, the frost had hardened it.

The horses were able to make light of the distance and the Britchka Chariot was well sprung.

In fact the Earl could not remember when he had last been in a vehicle that was so skilfully made.

He assumed that this was another present from Rustuss Groon.

If the horses went with it, it was impossible for him not to feel extremely grateful.

It was growing dark.

The shadows were lengthening by the time they reached Inch Village.

Benita had not said a word since they had left the Chapel.

The Earl thought he ought to point out to her the fact that they had reached his home, but he could not bring himself to do so.

He turned the horses in through the wrought-iron gates which needed painting.

They passed two lodges which were empty because they were too dilapidated to be habitable.

Then they were moving up the drive with its ancient oak trees on either side.

Through her veil Benita had her first glimpse of Inch Hall.

She had somehow expected it to be large, ugly and menacing.

Instead, to her astonishment, it had a fairylike quality about it.

She had no idea it was a fine example of the Italian architecture of Elizabeth's reign.

All she could see was the elegance and beauty of the domes and statues on the roof silhouetted against the sky.

There were flickering lights in an enormous number of windows.

In front of the house and behind it was a lake spanned by a stone bridge.

If Benita was surprised by the lights in the windows, so was the Earl.

For one ghastly second he thought the house was on fire.

Then he realised that almost every room must have lighted candles in it.

He wondered who could be responsible for such a display.

He had left yesterday very early to go to London.

There were in the house only his Batman and a couple who had been there in his father's time.

They were very old, but he had been unable to find a cottage in which they could retire.

They had therefore continued to stay on at the Big House.

To them he was still 'Young Master Garth'.

They had called him this ever since he had toddled to the kitchen to be given the sweetmeats they kept for him.

He could not imagine the Losnets or Hawkins his Batman lighting all those candles.

But who else could have done it?

It must have been on the orders of Rustuss Groon.

"I wonder what else he has waiting for me?" he thought grimly.

He resented the intrusion into his house of the man who had manipulated him into marrying his daughter.

Then he told himself that anything that was done was not to please him, but her.

The silent woman who was beside him with the veil over her face.

"I must look at her!" the Earl told himself. "I *have* to look at her!"

He thought that the moment would come when he

helped her from the Chariot.

He drew up the horses at the front door.

As he did so he saw that a red carpet had been laid down the steps.

Before he could take that in, the groom behind him had gone to the horses' heads.

Two footmen, wearing to his astonishment his own livery, were helping his Bride out of the Chariot.

By the time he had descended and walked round the Britchka to the steps she had reached the top of them.

The Earl followed her.

When he reached the front-door he found a middle-aged man with greying hair standing there wearing the clothes of a Butler.

He bowed to him.

"Welcome home, M'Lord! And may I on behalf of myself and the staff offer Your Lordship our most respectful congratulations!"

The Earl stared at him.

"Who are you?" he asked.

"I'm Bolton, your Butler, M'Lord, and I hope I shall be to Your Lordship's satisfaction. I was Butler to the late Duke of Cumbria until His Grace's sad death."

He knew the Duke of Cumbria had been one of the richest men in England.

Any servant who had been in his employment would certainly be extremely competent.

Because for the moment it was impossible for him to speak, Bolton continued:

"There's champagne in the Drawing-Room, M'Lord, and we've done our best to make things as comfortable for Your Lordship as possible."

Somewhat belatedly the Earl looked round for his Bride.

He realised that while he had been talking to Bolton she had followed a footman.

He had escorted her up the stairway.

He could see that at the top of them there was a woman dressed in black.

Incredible though it seemed, he knew she was his Housekeeper.

There was nothing he could do but take a last glance at the figure wrapped in fur.

She turned to walk along the passage.

There was just a flash from the diamonds in her tiara before she disappeared.

Bolton was opening the door to the Drawing-Room.

As if he was hypnotised, the Earl walked across the hall and into the room he had never used since he had returned from France.

It had been his mother's favourite room.

He could not bear to see the marks on the walls from which he had removed the gold-framed mirrors.

He had also sold several pictures which were not entailed, and could therefore go to the Auctioneers.

Now to his astonishment the chandeliers had been lit.

Although the walls were bare, there were flowers in huge vases.

There was a fire burning in a grate which had been cleaned and polished.

Bolton went to a table in the corner.

The Earl could see a bottle of champagne standing in a silver wine-cooler.

It had obviously been taken out of the safe and was engraved with his crest.

It was entailed like all the rest of the silver, and he had therefore been unable to sell it.

As if he was in a dream, the Earl accepted the glass

Bolton handed him on a silver salver.

There were also some pâté sandwiches, and he took one.

"I hope you'll understand, My Lord," Bolton was saying, "that we have at the moment only a skeleton staff. But I have made some enquiries in the village."

He paused and then continued.

"I understand there're a number of young women anxious to work in the house, and plenty of young men looking for employment."

"I am – aware of that," the Earl managed to say.

"I've already taken on two of the most likely lads," Bolton continued, "and with Your Lordship's permission would like to have two more in the hall."

The Earl drank some champagne because he felt he needed it.

"The Chef," Bolton went on, "has brought one assistant with him, M'Lord, but he's only temporary. So if we take on two scullions in the kitchen, we could take on a third as soon as there's a place for him."

The Earl realised that Bolton was expecting an answer.

In a voice that did not sound like his own he said:

"Yes, yes, of course. I am sure you are doing your best in what for the moment are very uncomfortable circumstances."

"I was told, M'Lord," Bolton said, "that things have gone to rack an'ruin while Your Lordship was fighting so gallantly in Spain, and may I say that the staff are very proud to be in your employment."

"Thank you," the Earl said feeling somewhat embarrassed.

Bolton looked at the clock.

"If it pleases you, M'Lord, dinner'll be served in an hour's time. Mr. Hawkins, Your Lordship's Valet, has been extremely co-operative in helping us all settle in."

Bolton bowed and with a dignified walk, which would have graced a Member of the House of Lords, withdrew.

The Earl felt as if it was difficult to breathe and even more difficult to think.

Could this really be happening, or was it just an illusion?

He poured himself another glass of champagne and wished Sir Anthony was with him.

As the thought came to his mind he remembered that he had not yet seen or spoken to his wife.

He felt as if a cold hand touched his heart.

It was one thing to be bemused by what Rustuss Groon had arranged.

It was quite another to remember that he had not yet seen his wife.

He was vividly aware of her as he went up the stairs to his own room.

It was where the Earls of Inchester had slept since the house had first been built.

It was a magnificent room with an enormous four-poster bed draped in crimson velvet.

The Inchester Coat-of-Arms with its many quarterings was embroidered on the headboard.

The velvet was faded and the lining was torn.

Still the room had a grandeur and was to the Earl re-dolent with the history of those who had occupied it before him.

Before he reached the door he could not help thinking of the woman who was occupying the next room.

It had been his mother's.

As he passed by he could hear voices.

It made him move a little quicker, almost as if they were reaching out to stop him.

When he went into his own room he found Hawkins.

Because he was so glad to see a familiar face he involuntarily held out his hand to him.

"Congratulations, M'Lord!" the Valet said. "And may th'blessing o'Heaven be upon you, which be what Yer Lordship deserves."

The words came, the Earl knew, from Hawkins' warm heart.

Then he said in his usual cheeky manner:

"This be a nice 'ow-do'y-do, M'Lord, an' no mistake!"

"What has happened?" the Earl asked.

Hawkins was helping him out of his smart coat cut by Weston.

"As soon as Yer Lordship left yes'day morning, M'Lord, they arrives like a swarm o'bees!"

The Earl was listening as he undid his waist-coat.

"They comes in carriages, vans an'brakes! Yer Lordship 'as never seen such a carry on!"

Hawkins laughed.

"I kept pinchin' meself t'make sure Oi were still awake!"

"I am sure you did," the Earl said. "I am feeling rather the same."

"Now, all yer 'as to do, M'Lord, is t'sit back an' enjoy it. Everyone as comes 'ere 'as their instructions, an' knows 'ow to carry 'em out!"

The Earl thought he had no wish for people to be given instructions by somebody else in his own house.

But he did not interrupt and Hawkins went on:

"The Chef, an' believe it or not, 'e's a 'Froggy', can cook better than any man or woman I've ever met in me 'ole life!"

The Earl smiled.

He was sure this was true.

"Oi sez to 'im, I sez: 'For five years I've bin fightin' the loiks o' you. Wot am I supposed t'say t'ye now?' "

"What did he say?" the Earl asked in an amused voice.

" 'E sez: 'Open yer mouth an' eat this an' then ye'll know why I am here!' "

The Earl laughed.

It seemed a moment to remove a little of his tension.

He had noticed when he came into the room that a bath was arranged in front of the fire.

Huge brass cans of hot and cold water had been brought upstairs, and they had been polished.

For the moment he was content not to ask questions.

He enjoyed the warmth of the fire and the water.

There was no doubt from the excited note in Hawkins' voice that he, at any rate, was enjoying every moment of the upheaval.

When the Earl was dressed in his evening-clothes Hawkins said:

"Now, if yer don't enjoy yer dinner, M'Lord, an' think 'tis somethin' as 'as dropped down out o'the'sky, then Oi'll eat me 'at!"

The Earl laughed as he left the room.

He glanced at the door of his wife's bedroom and stopped himself from hurrying past it.

Downstairs a fire was blazing in the hall which he had not noticed when he came in.

Bolton was waiting in the Drawing-Room with a glass of champagne.

He noticed there was only one.

Before he could ask questions, Bolton said:

"I was told to make apologies to Your Lordship, but Her Ladyship is still asleep. Her old Nurse, who has come here to look after her, thinks it would be a mistake to waken her."

The Earl was almost ashamed of the sense of relief that seeped over him.

"Yes, of course." he said. "If Her Ladyship is asleep on no account is she to be woken. It has been a long day, and I am sure she must be very tired."

Bolton bowed and left the room.

He returned a few minutes later to announce in stentorian tones:

"Dinner is served, M'Lord!"

If the Earl had been surprised on arriving at Inch Hall so was Benita.

Because she was so ashamed of her tear-stained face and swollen eyes she had hurried up the stairs.

She felt she must go to her room before she spoke to her husband.

The Housekeeper who met her at the top of the stairs curtsied and said:

"Welcome Y'Ladyship! If you'll come this way I'll show Y'Ladyship the room in which you'll be sleeping."

She walked ahead and opened a door.

Benita walked in, then gave a cry that seemed to echo round the walls.

"Nanny!" she exclaimed. "Nanny! I had no idea that you would be here!"

She ran across the room and flung her arms round the elderly woman who was standing by the dressing-table.

When Benita was eighteen her Nanny, who had been with her since a baby, was nearly seventy.

She did not leave the Manor House where she had always been very happy.

But she did hand over her duties to a young maid, supervising her to make sure Benita had everything she wanted.

Major Grenfel had asked her to go to Inch Hall with the

luggage.

Nanny knew he was thinking she would help Benita to feel less homesick and lost without him.

"Of course I'll go, Sir," she said. "I'll not have any baby feeling she's alone with a lot of strange faces."

"I thought you would feel like that, Nanny, Major Grenfel replied, "and I want you to be with her when she is told that I am dead."

"Now don't you go talking like that, Sir," Nanny admonished.

Then as she saw the expression on her Master's face she had stopped.

"I'm right sorry, Sir, that I am! You knows what I feels about you, and your kindness to us all."

"The only thing that matters is Miss Benita," Major Grenfel said quietly. "You must make her undersand, Nanny, that she is not to grieve, and on no account is she to wear black!"

He was silent for a moment. Then he said:

"Make her realise that I am still alive and with her mother. I will be thinking of her and loving her as I have every day and every moment since she was born."

"I knows that, Sir," Nanny said, "and no child could have had a more devoted father."

"I can only say, Nanny," Major Grenfel added, "that I am very thankful that you are still with us."

It was obvious to Nanny as Benita clung to her that she was frightened.

As the Housekeeper shut the door and they were alone, Nanny said:

"Now, come along, dear and let me get you out of your finery so that you can have a rest."

Benita had dropped her fur cloak as she ran across the room.

Now Nanny began to take off her tiara and veil.

As she saw Benita's face she stifled a little exclamation and went to the door.

She spoke to someone outside and came back.

She was putting Benita into her nightgown when there was a knock.

Nanny went to the door.

She came back with a tray on which there was a jug of chocolate.

"Now you get into bed," she said, "and I'll give you some chocolate. Just what you enjoyed as a child."

"I could not eat much . . luncheon," Benita murmured.

Nanny took the chocolate to the wash-hand-stand.

"I've added a little honey," she said. "Now drink it up and have a nice sleep."

"I . . I shall have to . . go down to d . . dinner," Benita said in a frightened voice.

"Yes, of course," Nanny agreed soothingly, "but there's a time for everything, so just shut your eyes, and when you wakes up I've lots of things to tell you."

It was just like being back in the Nursery, Benita thought.

Nanny was there and nothing could harm or frighten her.

She seemed to have lived a hundred years since her father had told her she was to be married.

She was in fact exhausted.

Even quicker than Nanny had hoped, she had fallen into a deep sleep.

She slept on and on, as Nanny hoped she would.

Although she would not have admitted it, as well as the honey, Nanny had put herbs into the chocolate.

To Nanny's mind, it was quite wrong that Benita had

been rushed to the altar.

She had now seen the dilapidated state of Inch Hall.

She knew shrewdly exactly why the Earl wished to marry the child she loved.

"If it's money he's after," she said to herself, "he's got it right enough! But I'll not have him upsetting my baby, not for all the tea in China!"

If the Earl had been aware it was Nanny who had ensured that Benita did not join him for dinner, he would have been amused.

It was a great relief to him.

The dinner itself was superlative and the silver from the safe was polished and on the table.

There was also a decoration of white flowers to celebrate his wedding.

He thought it was the best meal he had ever eaten in his own home.

The wines too were superlative and could not, he knew, have come from his empty cellar.

He went back to the Drawing-Room to sit in front of the well-made-up fire and look at the newspapers.

Bolton had produced them like a conjurer before he said:

"I trust, M'Lord, everything is to Your Lordship's satisfaction. To-morrow we'll work on Your Lordship's Study, and the next day the Library."

"Thank you," the Earl said feeling there was nothing else he could say.

"I think I should inform Your Lordship that the workmen are arriving to-morrow morning to start on the house."

The Earl started.

"Another gang," Bolton went on, "are moving into the village to repair the cottages for the pensioners."

The Earl stared at the Butler as if he could not have heard him right.

"I'm sure Your Lordship will wish to see the Overseer after breakfast," Bolton continued, "and he's informed me that he'll be waiting on Your Lordship at nine o'clock."

Bolton left the room.

Only when he had gone did the Earl make a sound that was half an exclamation and half a note of triumph.

He could not believe it!

The whole thing was incredible.

But he had to admit that it was what he had always wanted.

What he had worked for these past years only to fail.

Now Rustuss Groon, of all people, had waved a magic wand and it was happening – actually happening!

He thought he could hardly wait for the night to pass.

He wanted to see the pensioners' faces when they found their cottages were being repaired.

When he told them that their pensions were to be trebled.

Then, almost as if it had slipped his memory, he remembered that this was his wedding-night.

His wedding night – and he had not yet spoken to his Bride!

He had not heard her voice except in a whisper when she had promised to obey him.

Was it likely she would do so when she had so much to give him, but he had nothing for her?

It was a sobering thought.

Because he was tired after the exertions of last night, he thought he would go to bed.

He reached the landing and drew near to the room in which Benita was sleeping.

He thought again that this was his wedding night.

He was obviously a very reluctant Bridegroom.

"At least," he argued with himself, "I should say goodnight to her. If she is awake she will think it unnecesarily rude on my part not to do so."

With an effort therefore he stopped outside Benita's bedroom and stared at the door.

If he had nothing personal to give his wife, he could at least be courteous and grateful.

He knocked very gently.

He heard no reply and turned the handle.

The door was locked.

CHAPTER FIVE

Benita woke early and for a moment could not think where she was.

Then she saw that above the curtains which covered the window the paper was torn away from the wall.

There were heavy stains on the painted ceiling.

With a start she remembered that yesterday she had been married.

She looked at the gold clock beside her bed which her father had given her.

It was after seven o'clock.

She got out of bed and drew back the curtains.

The sun was rising but there were still a few stars left in the sky overhead.

There was the sparkle of frost on the grass and the boughs of the trees were still.

Benita thought the wind that had been so cold yesterday had dropped.

"I will go riding," she decided.

Nanny was in the house but she did not wish to wake her so early.

Instead she dressed herself in one of her riding-habits which she found in the wardrobe.

She put on two stiff petticoats under her skirt.

She never wore a hat when there was nobody to see her.

Now she tied back her long fair curls with a bow of silk ribbon.

Then without looking in the mirror she ran across the room to the door.

She was surprised to find it locked, but the key was on the inside.

She thought Nanny must have locked it last night and left through the *Boudoir* which was on one side of it.

However she did not want to think about anything but reaching the stables.

She went down the stairs.

She saw that two housemaids in mob-caps were already brushing the rugs in the hall and cleaning out the fire.

She smiled at them as they bobbed her a curtsy.

She went to the front-door which had already been unbolted.

Letting herself out she walked away in the direction the Britchka Chariot had gone yesterday evening after they arrived.

She was not mistaken and walking through an archway she saw a cobbled yard.

At the side there was a whole row of stables.

There were gaping holes on the roof of some of them and the doors were badly in need of paint.

Then as she walked towards the first one a groom came out and she recognised him.

It was Benny who looked after her father's horses, especially *Swallow*.

"Marnin', Miss B..Oi means Yer Ladyship! Oi comes 'ere yes'day wiv *Swallow*."

"With *Swallow*?" Benita exclaimed. "Do you mean he is here? Oh, Benny, how wonderful!"

"We arroived late-like," Benny explained. "Oi took'm easy 'cross country, so th'journey wouldn't take 'im long."

Benita was hardly listening.

She was hurrying into the stables to where in the first stall there was *Swallow*.

"You are here! You are here, *Swallow*!" she exclaimed. "I am so very happy to see you!"

She put her arms around his neck and hugged him.

Benny was fetching a saddle.

As he fastened the girths he said:

"There be some foin 'orses 'ere, Miss.. Oi means M'Lady, but th'stables be in a terrible state!"

"I am sure you will see that *Swallow* is comfortable," Benita murmured.

Benny led the horse outside to the mounting-block and she seated herself on the saddle.

Then she was riding away feeling that nothing mattered except that she had *Swallow* with her.

Anything unpleasant could wait until she returned from her ride.

She went over fields that had not been ploughed but were perfect for galloping.

She went still further and saw ahead some rough hedges.

If there was one thing *Swallow* enjoyed it was jumping, and she took him at them.

He leapt them one after the other with nearly a foot to spare.

"That was splendid, *Swallow*!" Benita exclaimed.

"You are a very good boy!"

She bent forward to pat his neck.

When she straightened herself again she saw to her surprise somebody was riding towards her.

It was a man and she had a feeling, although she was not sure, that it was the Earl.

She had never looked at him during the Service or as they walked down the aisle.

But when they were driving towards Inch Hall she had glanced at him nervously once or twice.

But by that time it was growing dusk and she could only have a vague glimpse of his profile.

As he came nearer she drew in her breath.

The Earl swept off his hat.

"Good-morning!" he said. "I have been admiring the way your horse took those fences like a bird!"

Benita gave a little laugh.

"His name is *Swallow*, so your compliment is very apt!"

"*Swallow?*" the Earl replied. "That is a coincidence, for the horse I am riding is called *Hawk!*"

Benita looked at the very large black stallion on which he was astride.

She was aware the horse was very badly groomed.

At the same time it was a majestic-looking animal, if not particularly well-bred.

"I ought to apologise for the fact that he is not looking as smart as *Swallow*," the Earl said, "but there has only been myself to look after him and I have not been a particularly conscientious groom!"

Benita smiled.

She was suddenly aware that the Earl – and she was sure it was he – did not know who she was.

His next words told her she was right.

"I think you must be staying in this part of the country," he observed, "for I have never seen you before."

Benita smiled again.

She could not help thinking it was an amusing situation.

This was the man she had married yesterday afternoon, and of whom she had been so afraid.

He was certainly very good-looking. The most handsome man she had ever met.

And he thought she was a stranger!

"I want you to tell me more about *Hawk*," she said. "Did you buy him?"

"I could not afford to," he replied. "He was given to me six months ago because no one could handle him."

"And you have taught him how to behave?"

"He is still a little troublesome with anybody else, but he has acknowledged after a great number of battles that I an his master."

Benita laughed.

"I think really," she said, "that you love him. My father has always said that the only way to tame a horse is to love him so much that he wants to obey you."

"I have never thought of it that way before," the Earl laughed, "but I am sure your father is right."

He thought as she smiled at him that she was the most beautiful person he had ever seen.

He was racking his brains to think where and with whom she could be staying in the neighbourhood.

The Lord Lieutenant was very old and he had never known him to give house-parties for young people.

Since the War his immediate neighbours all seemed to be over fifty.

If their sons and daughters were alive they spent their time in London.

"I see another hedge ahead of us," Benita exclaimed. "If you will give *Swallow* a little start because he is smaller than *Hawk*, I will race you."

"I will count to ten slowly," the Earl said, "and there are two more fences beyond that one."

Benita touched *Swallow* lightly with her whip.

The Earl started counting so that she was able to put a good distance between them.

Then he gave *Hawk* his head and the great stallion did exactly what was expected of him.

Benita had jumped the first fence before the Earl reached her.

Then they were side by side for the second but *Hawk* was a length ahead at the third.

The Earl pulled in the stallion and waited for Benita to catch up with him.

There were curls round her forehead and a bright colour in her cheeks.

She looked so exquisite that it was difficult for him to believe she was real.

Never in the lonely rides which he took every morning had he ever encountered anyone.

Certainly not a goddess from Olympus.

"You won!" Benita said as she reached him. "But *Hawk* has got much longer legs!"

"He would have been extremely mortified if he had been beaten by a small *Swallow*!" the Earl replied.

They both laughed.

There was a wood ahead of them.

Benita realised that after a long ride round they were now quite near the house again.

As if the Earl read her thoughts he said:

"I think perhaps you ought to return to wherever you have come from. I am only afraid that if it is to the moon or Mount Olympus I cannot accompany you to either!"

Benita laughed.

"No, it is nearer than that."

The Earl hesitated.

"I suppose you would not like to have breakfast with me? My house is not far away and I am sure so much jumping has aroused your appetite!"

"You are quite right, I *am* hungry," she said, "and I am delighted to accept your invitation."

She remembered as she spoke that she had missed dinner last night.

And at luncheon she had been too perturbed, after her father had told her she was to be married, to eat anything.

She was aware that the Earl had hesitated before inviting her to breakfast.

She knew perceptively that it was because he had remembered his wife.

He was wondering if she might object to his entertaining a visitor while she was still in bed.

Actually the Earl had thought of his wife.

It crossed his mind that the contrast between her and this exquisite young woman might prove somewhat uncomfortable.

Then he had told himself that she had been too tired to dine with him last night.

She would therefore not be rising early this morning and there should be no difficulty.

He was not prepared to admit that he had no wish to lose so quickly this apparition of beauty who had suddenly graced his barren land.

They started to ride back towards Inch Hall, taking several jumps on the way.

Then they settled down to a comfortable trot across

the fields which had not been cultivated.

"It is very beautiful here," Benita remarked as she looked around her.

"It could be," the Earl agreed, "but while I was away at the War nothing was done and everything has run wild."

"You were in the War?" Benita asked.

"I was," the Earl replied, "and after Waterloo I came home to find worse devastation on my estate that I had seen on the battlefield!"

He spoke with a bitterness which was very revealing.

Knowing her father's feelings about the horrors of War and the privations of peace, Benita understood.

Slowly in her own mind the puzzle of her marriage was beginning to fall into place.

She could understand already why her father had chosen the Earl for her husband.

She felt, however, it was far easier to meet him while he thought she was a stranger.

Ingenuously she asked:

"Is that your house we can see in the distance? It looks very lovely!"

"It could be," the Earl said, "and it was when I was a child, but now.."

He stopped, feeling it was a mistake to say any more.

He merely added:

"I would like you to see it one day when I get it back to what it was originally."

"I think it is beautiful now."

She was speaking sincerely.

The morning sun was shining on the almost white bricks and the windows were shining like diamonds.

Her spirits were rising.

It was almost as if her father was beside her with his

eyes twinkling, because he had surprised her.

The Earl was very different from what she had expected.

She had never seen a more handsome man.

She was aware too that he rode magnificently and seemed part of his horse.

They drew nearer to what she now thought was a Fairy Palace.

She was aware as they did so that the Earl was looking up at the roof.

There were a number of men moving about on it, and he knew the workmen had arrived.

They drew their horses to a standstill outside the front door.

Two grooms were waiting for them.

One was Benny.

He was just about to speak when Benita put her finger to her lips.

He looked surprised, but he was quick-witted enough to understand.

He merely grinned as he took hold of *Swallow's* bridle.

"Come in!" the Earl invited.

Benita followed him up the steps.

Bolton was not in the hall, but there were two footmen on duty.

"We want breakfast immediately!" the Earl ordered.

"It's ready, M'Lord in t'Breakfast-Room," one of the footmen replied.

He went ahead to open the door for them.

It led into a room which the Earl had not entered for at least six months.

It had been a favourite room of his mother's because it had the early morning sun.

With only himself in the house there had seemed no

reason to use more rooms than was absolutely necessary.

The Breakfast-Room had been left with its shutters closed, the dust accumulating.

Now it looked very different.

There was a lace edge linen cloth on the table.

Just as in his father's day, the food was in silver entree dishes which stood over lighted candles to keep it warm.

There was a selection of six to choose from as well as a whole ham and a large brawn on a side-table.

"Come and tell me what you would like to eat," the Earl suggested.

"I warn you I am very hungry!" Benita replied.

"If there is not enough here," he said, "we can always send for more!"

They both laughed because there was enough food on the side-board for at least a dozen people.

Benita chose a small trout which she suspected had just been caught in the lake, and some scrambled eggs.

The Earl filled his plate with lambs' kidneys and a number of other dishes.

While they were choosing, a footman brought in a silver coffee jug and a tea-pot.

The servants withdrew and the Earl knew it was on Bolton's orders.

Obviously, like his father, the Duke of Cumbria had preferred to have breakfast without being surrounded by servants.

They sat down and the Earl looked at Benita and almost forgot to eat.

Because it had made her hot to ride so strenuously she took off the jacket of her habit and put it on a chair.

She was wearing a very pretty muslin blouse inset with lace.

It had a small bow of blue ribbon at the neck which

matched the bow in her hair.

With her fair hair streaming down her back she might have been a schoolgirl, the Earl thought.

Then as he saw the rounded curves of her breasts beneath the blouse he knew she was very much a woman.

"Now," he began, "you must tell me all about yourself."

Benita smiled.

"I feel a formal introduction would be banal."

"What do you mean by that?" he asked.

"I cannot believe that Perseus, after he had killed the dragon, immediately asked the Princess he had saved to identify herself!"

The Earl laughed.

"What you are saying is that I should either know who you are, or should be clever enough to guess!"

"And I will of course give you a prize if you are successful," Benita laughed.

"I want your prize – I want it very much!" the Earl said. "But for the life of me I cannot imagine why you should be tresspassing on my land, or from where you can possibly have come."

As he spoke, he thought again of his neighbours.

He could not think who could be entertaining anyone so entrancing.

Benita finished what she was eating and helped herself from a honey-comb.

She spread it on some bread which had been freshly baked.

As the Earl was silent, she asked:

"Have you solved the problem?"

He shook his head and said:

"Promise me that you will not vanish and leave me afraid that I have lost you forever!"

"It would make a romantic ending if you went day after day to the hedges we have just left to look for me."

"Can you imagine anything more frustrating if you never come back?" the Earl asked.

Benita had finished her breakfast.

"I wonder," she said, "if I could go upstairs and tidy myself before I leave?"

"But of course!" the Earl replied. "I should have asked you before if that was what you would like to do."

He rose to his feet, as he did so ringing a silver bell that stood on the table beside him.

The door opened immediately.

"Will you take this young lady up to the House-keeper?" he asked.

As he spoke he realised, and he thought it was amusing, that he knew neither the name of his guest, nor that of his Housekeeper.

Benita left the room and he walked into the hall.

He looked along the passage which led towards the Study.

He saw, as Bolton had promised, servants carrying buckets, brushes and dustpans going to clean it.

He went into the Drawing-Room where he had sat last night.

He appreciated that the windows had been opened and a fire was burning in the fireplace.

There seemed to be even more flowers than there had been yesterday.

He walked to the window to stand looking out into the garden.

There were four gardeners working away at the overgrown shrubs, the undug flower-beds and the lawn which had become virtually a hayfield.

They were all local men from the village.

He told himself once again that he should be very grateful to Rustuss Groon.

Then he remembered that Groon's daughter was sleeping upstairs.

He turned from the window, and as if he suddenly felt cold he went towards the fire.

Benita ran the length of the passage to her own room.

She found, as she expected, that Nanny was there.

"I guessed you'd gone riding, Mi..M'Lady!" Nanny said.

"Quick! Quick!" Benita cried. "I want to change! I will tell you why later."

Nanny undid the blouse and brought from the wardrobe one of the exceedingly pretty and expensive gowns which had come from London.

Benita sat down at the dressing-table.

Nanny skilfully twisted her hair into a *chignon* at the back of her head.

"It wants brushing," Nanny said.

"We can do that later," Benita answered. "I must go downstairs again – now!"

She spoke so urgently that Nanny did not ask any questions.

Putting the last pin in her hair Benita rose to her feet.

"I will come back and explain later," she promised as she ran across the room.

Downstairs she found Bolton in the hall.

"Good-morning, M'Lady!" he said.

"Where is His Lordship?" Benita asked softly.

"His Lordship's in the Drawing-Room, M'Lady," Bolton replied, "as the Study's not yet ready."

"Please see that we are not disturbed until I ring,"

Benita said.

She did not look to see if there was an expression of surprise on Bolton's pontifical face.

She ran to the door of the Drawing-Room and before he could open it she went in.

The Earl was standing at the mantlepiece looking down into the fire.

As he heard her enter he turned round eagerly.

Then there was an expression of astonishment in his eyes as he saw how she was dressed.

Slowly she walked towards him, watching him as she did so.

When she reached him she dropped him a small curtsy.

"Well?" she questioned. "Have you an answer to the problem, or are you prepared to admit defeat?"

"I – do not understand," the Earl said. "How have you managed to change – unless you are staying in my house?"

It passed through his mind that she might be a friend of his wife's.

Then as he saw she was laughing at him, an idea came to him.

It was so incredible, so absolutely absurd, that he thought he must be a fool even to think it.

"You are – not.." he began. "You could not be..?"

He stopped.

"Go on," Benita prompted.

"It is not possible for you to.."

Again he could not say the words.

"I think you are being cowardly." Benita said, "or else you have failed to guess the right answer. All right – I will give it to you!"

She curtsied as she said:

"I am, My Lord, your wife!"

The Earl gave an audible gasp.

His brain told him that there must be some mistake, or else this lovely young woman was playing a joke on him.

Perhaps that was the real answer.

It might be her idea of fun, or even Rustuss Groon's.

Either way, somebody was contriving to make him look a fool.

"You – say you are – my wife," he said slowly, the words seeming to force themselves from his lips. "In which case – what is your name?"

"Benita Grenfel, at your sevice!"

Now the Earl thought he understood.

This was a trick, and Rustuss Groon had no daughter.

He had married him to some woman whose father was in debt to him, and who wanted an aristocrat for his son-in-law.

He could see the plot quite clearly.

However he had no intention of being rude to the lovely creature who was looking at him tentatively.

Instead he said with a smile:

"It is – impossible for you to be – any relation to – Rustuss Groon!"

Benita looked puzzled.

"That is a strange name! And you are right in thinking he is no relation of mine!"

The Earl smiled at his own cleverness more than because he felt amused.

"Are you telling me the truth when you say that we are married?" he asked.

"You cannot have forgotten the little Chapel and the Parson who joined us!"

She held up her left hand.

"You placed my mother's wedding-ring on my finger, and it was then I knew that nothing would be as horrifying as I had imagined!"

"You did not – wish to marry me?" the Earl asked.

"No, of course not!" she answered. "I could not believe it was true when Papa told me yesterday morning that I was to be married in the afternoon!"

She gave a little shiver and looked at the fire.

"I..I was very..frightened..and I wanted to..run away."

"And yet you came to the Chapel!"

The Earl thought his brain was once again whirling as it had in Rustuss Groon's office.

"My..father is..very ill." Benita explained in a low voice, "and I could not..refuse anything he..asked of me."

"What is your father's name?"

Benita looked at him in surprise.

"Surely you know?"

"I just want to make sure I have got it right," the Earl replied.

"My father is Major Richard Grenfel..and the..kindest and most wonderful man in the whole world!"

There was a note of agony in her voice which the Earl did not miss.

"You say he is ill?" he asked.

"Yes, very," Benita replied, "and please..please will you take me over to see him..as soon as you can?"

"Yes, of course I will do anything you want," the Earl answered, "but I still do not understand."

As he spoke he thought he had no wish to upset this lovely child, for she was little more.

Then he added quickly:

"What I meant to say was – I cannot understand how I am so fortunate, being married in such a strange way, to find myself married to you!"

Benita smiled.

"Do you mean..that?"

"I mean it," he said. "And you ride better than any woman I have ever met."

"Now you are complimenting *Swallow* and I am sure he appreciates it!"

The Earl laughed. Then he said:

"I think, Benita, this is very exciting! We can get to know each other and let us pretend, instead of being married in that peculiar manner without having met before, we have only met by chance out riding."

Benita laughed too, and it was a very pretty sound.

"That would be a lovely game to play, and I must of course apologise to Your Lordship for trespassing on your land!"

"Everything I have is yours!" the Earl said using a phrase.

As he spoke he knew that was true.

But he thought it was something he did not wish to remember for the moment.

Instead he said:

"You said you are interested in my house, so I hope that you will stay long enough to inspect it, and see what is being done to it at the moment."

Benita clasped her hands together.

"I would love to do that! Shall we start from the roof and go downwards, or the cellars and go up?"

"We will do both!"

He glanced at the clock.

"But first I have the Overseer who is coming to see me at nine o'clock, and I suggest we see him together."

"Do you really want me, or would you rather see him alone?"

"I think, since what the workmen are doing will

concern us both, you should also make some of the decisions."

"That is an exciting idea!" Benita said. "Let us start at once!"

She spoke with a childlike enthusiasm.

"I will find out if he is here," the Earl said and walked towards the door.

As he went he told himself that something very peculiar was going on.

He was determined to get to the bottom of it sooner or later.

For the moment, however, as Benita was obviously as ignorant as he was, he would have to 'play it by ear'.

"I might have known that Rustuss Groon would deceive me in one way or another!" he told himself.

As he reached the door he felt an unutterable relief.

His wife was not the ugly, bearlike creature he had expected her to be.

Instead she was somebody lovely and so fascinating.

He looked back at Benita to see that she was still in the room and had not vanished when he walked away from her.

She was there, and smiling.

He smiled back before he opened the door to ask Bolton if the Overseer had arrived.

CHAPTER SIX

The Overseer was full of surprises.

He informed the Earl that he had taken on a large number of local men to repair the house.

"I thought, M'Lord," he said, "we'd start at the top as the roof's in pretty bad shape."

"I am aware of that," the Earl said quietly.

"I've arranged, if it suits Your Lordship, for the painters to arrive this afternoon to discuss with Your Lordship the colours you want in the various rooms."

The Earl nodded and glanced at Benita.

He saw she was listening attentively to everything the Overseer said.

"We've got the best gold-leaf Artist in London coming down later, M'Lord, to touch up the ceilings, the pelmets and of course some of the furniture."

"I am sure when you have finished it will look as it did in my grandfather's time," the Earl remarked.

"I should imagine," Benita said unexpectedly, "that if we look in the Library we will find the sketches and designs which were made when the house was first built."

She paused to look at the Earl and then she continued:

"It would be wonderful if you used the same colours as the Architect chose then."

The Earl thought this was a very intelligent idea and so did the Overseer.

He went on to explain what was being done in the village.

The Earl decided the sooner he went to see the pensioners himself the better.

When the Overseer left them, he was just about to suggest this to Benita when Nanny came hurrying into the room.

She was carrying what looked like a parcel.

As she reached the Earl she said:

"I can only say how sorry I am, M'Lord, but it slipped m'memory, what with a'coming here so fast, and putting Mi..Her Ladyship to bed, I never gave it another thought!"

"Gave what?" the Earl asked.

"The Master says to me before I leaves, he says: 'Now, Nanny, put this parcel into His Lordship's hands, and give it to nobody else.' "

The Earl took what she was holding and knew what it was.

"This is something I am very grateful to have, Nanny!" he said.

"Then that's all right, M'Lord. I was also to tell Your Lordship, that Captain Dawson'll be coming over to-morrow morning."

She did not wait for the Earl to reply, but turned to Benita and said:

"Will you be coming upstairs, M'Lady, so that I can arrange your hair better?"

"I will come in a few minutes, Nanny,' Benita answered.

Nanny left the room and Benita looked curiously at what the Earl was carrying to a *secretaire*.

"What has Papa sent you?" she asked.

"If it is what I think it is," the Earl replied, "it is very welcome."

Benita stood beside him as he opened the parcel.

There were a number of bags which the Earl was sure contained money.

Two carried sovereigns, two others which were larger contained silver.

There were also a number of notes of high value.

"Oh, it is money!" Benita exclaimed as if she was disappointed.

"It is money which is going to give a great deal of happiness and pleasure to people who very much deserve it," the Earl smiled.

She looked at him in surprise, and he said:

"Go upstairs and put on your bonnet and a warm coat, while I order a vehicle in which we can drive to the village."

She obeyed him without asking any questions.

When she had gone he looked at the money.

He could hardly believe it was not 'Fairy Gold' and would disappear if he touched it.

Then he found himself thanking Major Grenfel and Rustuss Groon.

He added a litle prayer of thankfulness that he was married to the most beautiful girl he had ever seen.

Not, as he had been afraid, to a woman who looked like Rustuss Groon.

"What is the truth about all this?" he asked as he put the larger notes into a drawer in the French *secretaire*.

It had belonged to his mother and being entailed he had not been able to sell it.

It was a very beautiful inlaid piece of furniture and he was glad now that it was in this room.

He knew it would be used by Benita.

He could imagine her sitting, as his mother had done, writing letters of thanks, or invitations to their neighbours.

He was aware that, contrary to what he had expected, he would be very proud of his wife.

He locked the drawer and put the key into his pocket.

As he did so he asked himself how he would ever be able to explain how she was so rich.

It was undoubtedly due to Rustuss Groon.

But if, as he had first thought, Major Grenfel was his client, then where was the money coming from?

"I do not understand," he said under his breath.

At the same time he was sure that Benita did not understand either.

"I must be very careful not to upset her," he decided.

He went out of the Drawing-Room into the hall.

He told Bolton to send to the stables immediately for a carriage to take them to the village.

Bolton looked out of the window as if to make sure that the weather was fine before he said:

"I wonder if Your Lordship'd like to try out the Phaeton?"

"A Phaeton?" the Earl exclaimed.

"It arrived from London yesterday afternoon, M'Lord," Bolton explained, "and I think it's the finest I've ever seen!"

"Then I would much like to try it," the Earl said.

As he spoke he felt his head was reeling.

Who was sending him all these things? Could it really

be Rustuss Groon?

But why if, as seemed evident, Benita was not his daughter?

"I do not understand," he said for the hundreth time.

Bolton gave instructions to one of the footmen who hurried away towards the stables.

He came towards the Earl.

"While Your Lordship was engaged with the Overseer," he said, "boxes arrived from Weston's by Post-Chaise. I've handed them over to Mr. Hawkins."

"From Weston's?" the Earl repeated beneath his breath.

He thought now nothing more could surprise him.

It was Rustuss Groon who had supplied him with his wedding-garments.

The Tailors had been right when they hinted there were more to come.

It suddenly struck him that perhaps Rustuss Groon did not want Benita to be ashamed of her husband.

Considering what he had felt about her before he met her, this was another joke at which he was forced to laugh.

Then he told himself that he should be annoyed.

He was being treated like a puppet on a string, not even allowed to think or do anything for himself.

Just for a moment he wanted to assert his authority and at least choose his own clothes.

Then he heard Benita speaking to him from the top of the stairs.

He looked up at her.

She was so lovely that he knew he did not want in contrast to look shabby and in rags.

"I am ready," Benita announced, "and you must admit I have been quick!"

"Very quick!" the Earl agreed.

She came down the stairs.

She was wearing a deep pink velvet coat trimmed down the front and round the hem with ermine.

A bonnet rimmed with the same fur was tied with satin ribbons under her chin.

She looked so exquisite as she reached him that he had an unrepressible impulse to kiss her.

Then as she looked up at him she asked:

"Where are we going?"

The Earl, who was staring at her in a bemused manner, called his thoughts to attention.

"One minute," he said, "I have to fetch something from the Drawing-Room."

A footman had helped him into his many-tiered over-coat which he had worn yesterday when they left the Chapel.

It had deep pockets.

Into the one on the left-hand side he put the bags containing the sovereigns.

Into the pocket on the other side he put the bags containing the silver.

The notes he slipped into an inside pocket.

Then he joined Benita.

She was looking at the Phaeton which had just come round from the stables.

Painted yellow with black wheels, it was drawn by a perfectly matched pair of jet black horses.

"You are right, Bolton," the Earl said, "it is the smar-test Phaeton I have ever seen!"

"I was sure Your Lordship'd appreciate it!" Bolton replied.

He helped Benita into the passenger-seat while the Earl picked up the reins.

The groom jumped up behind and they drove off.

With the sun shinning the Earl thought no man could tool a finer pair of horses.

Nor, for that matter, have a lovelier woman sitting beside him.

They reached the village which had once been very attractive.

Now the thatch on the black and white cottages was full of holes.

There were weeds growing on the thatch itself.

The gardens of the cottages were overgrown as if the occupants were too weak to make the effort to tend them.

The gates and fences were left unrepaired.

The broken panes in the windows had not been replaced, but blocked up with pieces of paper or rags.

The Earl was aware that as she looked at them Benita stifled a little cry of horror.

He himself felt as always a sense of shame and humiliation.

They drove into the centre of the village.

Workmen had already begun to strip the old thatch off the roof of one of the cottages.

Carpenters were replacing a dilapidated window-frame.

A new door was propped up against the fence waiting to be fitted into place.

There were not only workmen there, but also about a dozen of the inhabitants of the cottages watching.

The Earl drew his horses to a standstill.

Before he could alight from the Phaeton the villagers clustered around.

"Be it true, M'Lord," they asked, "as all our cottages t'be repaired?" "Will they be a-doin' mine?" "An'mine?"

"..An' mine?"

The voices rose excitedly and the Earl when he could make himself heard said:

"All your cottages are to be repaired and painted inside and out."

There was a cry of delight and he went on:

"If all of you who need new furniture and new beds will make a list of your requirements, I will see they are supplied to you as quickly as possible."

Now the babble of voices rose to a crescendo and the Earl added:

"I intend to call on each one of you in your cottages, but as most of you seem to be here, it is easier for me to tell you how sorry I am that things ever got to this stage. But now everything will be changed."

" 'Ow's that? Wot's 'appened, M'Lord?" one of the inhabitants shouted.

The Earl put out his hand to Benita who came round from the other side of the Phaeton to join him.

"First of all I would like to introduce you to my wife. She is anxious to meet you, as I am sure you are to meet her."

There was a gasp of surprise at this.

Benita walked round shaking hands with each one of the old pensioners.

The women bobbed her a curtsy and the men touched their foreheads.

While she was doing this, more and more people kept arriving.

The Earl calculated that the whole village, including the Butcher, the Baker and the Grocer were all there.

He shook hands with the three elderly men who had kept the shops ever since he was a boy.

"Wot be a-happenin', M'Lord?" one of them asked.

"Ye could'a knocked me down with a feather when Oi sees 'ow ye're repairing t'cottages!"

"I am also repairing the Big House," the Earl said, "and I am hoping to give employment to a large number of men on the land."

There was a shout of excitement at this from a number of men who had just joined the crowd.

The Earl knew most of them had served in the Army and Navy.

They had returned from the War to find the jobs they had had before they left were no longer available.

There were also a dozen or so young men.

They had grown up with nothing to do but idle about the village and poach in the neglected woods.

He walked now towards them.

"To-morrow," he said, "I want you to come and see me at about ten o'clock. We will then decide what work is available on the estate and what qualifications you have for various posts on the Farm, in the garden, the woods – and of course, the stables."

There was a glimmer of excitement in some of the younger men's eyes.

It told him that was where they wanted to be.

It flashed through his mind that it depended a great deal on how much money Benita actually had.

From what he himself had seen already and from what Rustuss Groon had told him, he knew she was rich.

But if everything he wanted to do was to be possible, she would need to be very rich indeed.

Benita had finished shaking hands with the old people and now she came to his side.

"I hope, my dear," he said as to include her in what he was saying, "that we can find employment for all these men on our estate."

"I am sure we can," Benita replied.

She then started to shake hands with the men and the boys.

The Earl went back to the old people and said in a quiet voice:

"I have brought some money with me to tide you over until Friday when from now on you will receive a bigger weekly pension."

There was a murmur as he went on:

"May I go into one of your cottages so that I can sit down? Then if you come in one by one, I will give you what I have with me."

"Me cottage b'ere, next door!" an old woman said.

"An' mine's on t'other side!" another one interrupted.

It was Mr. Greary, the Grocer, who had a better idea.

"Wot d'ye say, M'Lord," he suggested, "if ye sits inside me shop? Oi've a table there, an' more room than there'd be in one o'em cottages."

"That is very kind of you, Greary," the Earl said.

The shop was only a very short distance away.

As Mr. Greary led him towards it the pensioners followed him, the Earl thought, as if he was the Pied Piper.

They reached the door of the small shop with its bow window in which the glass needed repairing.

Benita joined him.

"I know what you are going to do," she said slipping her hand into his, "and may I help?"

The Earl smiled at her before he said:

"I could not manage without you, as you well know."

"It is so like Papa, to remember you would need money for your people as soon as you arrived."

The Earl had a sudden picture of Rustuss Groon slumped at his desk between two flickering candles in his dingy, dirty office off Piccadilly.

Because he did not wish to spoil the pleasure of this moment he thrust the memory from him.

Mr. Greary had pulled from the wall a small deal table so that the Earl could sit behind it.

By the time he had done so Benita was standing beside him.

The first of the old pensioners was coming in through the door and the rest were queuing up outside.

The Earl drew the bags of money from his pocket and put them down on the table.

He sorted out two sovereigns and a silver crown for each pensioner.

He arranged them in little piles.

Benita gave one to the old lady who had come in first.

She just stared at it as if she thought her eyes be deceiving her.

"Be this all for Oi?" she asked, "or be it for ever'one?"

"It is all for you, Mrs. Blackett," the Earl said, "to try and make up for short commons you have been on for so long."

As she turned to go he added:

"In future you will receive twelve shillings a week, every Friday."

"God bless ye, M'Lord! Oi never thought Oi's live t'see th'day!"

Her rheumaticky old hands closed over the money.

With tears running down her cheeks she moved to let the next pensioner take her place.

By the time everybody had been paid, their expressions of gratitude made Benita feel like crying herself.

The Earl put into the bag the few remaining sovereigns that were left.

She bent and whispered in his ear.

"Of course!" he said.

She turned to Mr. Greary who had been standing watching them from behind his counter.

"Please, Mr. Greary," she said, "will you give me pennies for two of these crowns?"

He pulled open the cash-drawer to find for her what she asked.

She had noticed while the old people were receiving their money a lot of very young boys were peering through the window.

They looked thin and their clothes were decidedly ragged.

Some of them, despite the cold, had bare feet.

She went out of the door as the Earl asked the men to come in.

As he was giving them a crown each, Benita gathered the small boys around her.

"I have two pennies for each of you," she said, "and I want you to promise me that you will spend them on something like a bun or a sausage roll."

She paused, looking round at them, and then continued:

"You must do that at once at the Baker's, and when you come back I will give you another penny with which to buy sweets from Mr. Greary."

There was a whoop of joy and they all ran off towards the Baker's shop.

It was a little further down the road.

Benita waited.

The first one back was a small boy who had in his hand a large piece of cheese between two pieces of bread.

"Oi buy it," he said.

"I see you have," Benita said, "and it was very sensible of you. Now you will not feel hungry, and I am sure to-night your mother will have something very good for you to eat."

Even as she spoke she wondered what they would have.

When she gave them all the third penny the Earl joined her.

The men to whom he had given a crown were extremely grateful.

He knew that most of them would be sensible enough to spend it on food rather than ale.

"They look so hungry," Benita said to the Earl in a low voice so that the boys could not hear, "and they are much too thin."

"I know," he said, "and that is why we are going to the Butcher's which is a little further down the village."

He took Benita's arm and they walked, followed by a crowd of small boys eating as they went.

They were afraid that if they stopped to spend their pennies at Mr. Greary's they would miss some of the fun.

The Butcher's shop was spotlessly clean but the Earl noticed the pathetically small stock of cheap cuts of meat.

There were one or two rabbits, which be suspected were poached and a few unplucked pigeons.

"I'm afraid I've nothin' much t'show Yer Lordship," the Butcher said apologetically.

"That is what I am going to speak to you about," the Earl replied. "I was thinking, Mr. Savage, perhaps you could get hold of a young ox."

Benita stared at him before he said:

"I'm sure I could do that, M'Lord, but it'll not be cheap."

The Earl put his hand into his inside pocket and drew out two notes.

"This should cover the cost and perhaps it would buy

two sheep as well."

"That it would, M'Lord!"

"Will you get hold of them as quickly as possible and divide the meat among all the families in the village?"

For a moment the Butcher seemed to have had his breath taken away. Then he said:

"It'll be th'first decent meal many of 'em 'ave 'ad for a long time!"

"I am aware of that," the Earl said, "but I promise you, it will not be the last!"

Driving back to Inch Hall Benita asked:

"How can people live in cottages that leak, and be so desperately cold all through the Winter?"

"That is what War does to the innocent," the Earl replied.

"They were so grateful because you thought of them."

"Of course I have thought of them," the Earl said, "but there was nothing I could do – nothing!"

As he spoke he thought that one day he would have to explain to Benita the reason why he had married her.

As if she was aware of it, to his surprise she said:

"It is all over now, and if you will employ those men and boys as quickly as possible, there will be no reason why anybody should go hungry."

The Earl was just about to say: "Not on my estate, at any rate!"

Then he bit back the words and said:

"Not on our estate!"

"I will help you to make that come true," Benita smiled.

"I will tell you what we will do," the Earl said. "As soon as the house is looking respectable again, we will give a party to celebrate our marriage."

Benita looked at him in surprise.

"Do you mean that?"

"We will invite the villagers, the Farmers, the tenants, and all our neighbours – why not?"

Benita laughed.

"I am sure it will be a very large party!"

"It is the way in which my father, my grandfather and my great-grandfather all celebrated their weddings," the Earl said. "We will roast an ox, and a stag, and have barrels and barrels of ale."

Benita laughed before she said:

"Could we please have fireworks? Papa has told me about the fireworks they have in Vauxhall Gardens, and I have always longed to see them."

"You have never seen fireworks?" the Earl asked.

Benita shook her head.

"Then we will have the best it is possible to obtain!" he said.

"That will be very exciting and I know the small boys will be thrilled."

It was luncheontime by the time they arrived home.

After they had eaten a delicious meal they went up onto the roof.

The workmen were busy there and they saw the Earl's standard which was flown when he was in residence.

It was in rags.

"We must get a new one at once!" Benita said.

"Perhaps we should keep this one to remind us to be careful with our money," the Earl replied, "in case it slips away, as it did when I was on the Continent."

"I am sure you need not be afraid of that," Benita answered. "Papa is so clever that he would never have lost a fortune as stupid young men do gambling and drinking."

The Earl could not help thinking that it was the gamblers and drinkers who had given Rustuss Groon his fortune.

It was also through Rustuss Groon that this money had come to him.

"You are looking very serious," Benita remarked, her voice intruding upon his thoughts.

"I am afraid I shall wake up and find that everything has vanished," the Earl said, "including you! I shall be standing all alone, looking at my tattered standard."

Benita laughed.

Then as she had done before she slipped her hand into his.

"I am still here," she said. "Now let us go find the painters and see how beautiful they are going to make the rooms of your house."

"*Our* house!" the Earl corrected. "And do not forget we must first find the original designs you thought of."

They actually found them late after tea when the painters had already started to decorate the Library.

It was Benita who found them pushed away at the back of a drawer.

"I have found them! I have found them!" she cried excitedly.

As the Earl turned them over he felt that not even Jason when he won back the Golden Fleece could have been so delighted.

"Now we can really make the house spectacular!" Benita said. "People will come from all over the country to admire it!"

"And you will be the most beautiful Countess the

Inchesters have ever had!" the Earl smiled.

The depth of sincerity in his voice made her glance at him in surpirse.

Then as her eyes met his she blushed and looked shy.

"You are very beautiful, Benita!" he said.

As he spoke he knew once again that he wanted to kiss her.

Although it seemed unlikely because she was so lovely, he was sure she had never been kissed.

He thought her lips would be different from those of any other woman he had ever known.

Of course there had been women in his life because he was so handsome.

They had pursued him and enticed him ever since he had left school.

But he had never felt really serious about any of what he thought of as his 'love-affairs'.

When he had gone to War, women had followed the Army during their slow, relentless advance in the Peninsula.

But they were not the type of woman a man would remember.

He knew by the quickening of his blood that to kiss Benita's perfectly shaped lips would be one of the most exciting experiences he had ever had.

Then he told himself that it was too soon.

He must be careful not to frighten her.

He was also aware of how very innocent and un-sophisticated she was.

She was playing the game he had suggested that they should meet as strangers.

Not yet as husband and wife.

He was aware there was an aura of purity about her.

It made her different from any other woman he had

ever known.

"I must make her love me first," he told himself.

Then he was astonished.

It was the last thing he had ever expected to want from Rustuss Groon's daughter.

They were finishing a candelit dinner seated at the dining-table.

Bolton had managed to arrange even more silver on it.

The Earl was wearing the extremely smart evening-clothes which had come to him from Weston's.

They fitted him as perfectly as the clothes that had been made for him to wear at his wedding.

How was it possible, he wondered, for Rustuss Groon to have found out his measurements so accurately.

"The man is definitely a Wizard," he told himself.

But he merely smiled at Hawkins as he remarked:

"Now, these, M'Lord, be wot I calls decent 'togs' for a Gent'man. Wot I can't understand, is 'ow they made 'em so quick when Yer Lordship was only in London th'day before yes'day!"

The Earl did not give Hawkins an answer because he did not know it himself.

He thought as he joined Benita in the Drawing-Room before dinner that his ancestors would be proud of them both. She was looking exquisitely lovely in a gown made of gauze.

It was embroidered all over with forget-me-nots and ribbons of the same colour crossed her breasts.

Bunches of forget-me-nots encircled the frill at the bottom of her gown.

There were little bunches of them on both sleeves.

"You look like Persephone,' he said, "come back from

the darkensss of Hell to bring a message of Spring to a poor mortal like me."

"Now you are being very poetic!" Benita said. "Shall I tell you that you look like a Greek God? Would you like to be Hermes or Apollo?"

Then she clapped her hands together and said:

"Oh, no, of course! I am quite wrong. You are Orion shining down from the sky on those beneath you who welcome your light in gold coins."

The Earl knew she was thinking of the pensioners and he laughed.

"Thank you, Benita. I am delighted to be Orion! But I feel if I am in the sky and you are on earth we are rather far apart."

There was a little pause before Benita said:

"Perhaps..we shall find a way of..getting a little closer."

The Earl drew in his breath.

Then before he could think of an answer Bolton had announced dinner.

He thought as the meal ended that his Chef got better and better.

Or was it because it was so delightful being with Benita that everything seemed enchanted?

Having left them with coffee and a small glass of brandy for the Earl, the servants withdrew.

Benita asked:

"Ought I to leave you? Mama always said it was correct."

"I do not want you to leave me now – or ever!" the Earl replied. "So you must wait until I have finished my brandy."

She smiled and suddenly without thinking he put out his hand towards her.

"Benita!" he said.

There was a different note in his voice from what there had been before.

She looked at him and he thought her eyes opened a little wider.

But before she could speak, suddenly a loud voice was shouting outside the Dining-Room door.

Both the Earl and Benita stiffened.

A moment later the door was flung open and a footman said nervously:

"Lord Shaptill, M'Lord!"

As he spoke a man strutted into the room.

In the same loud and angry voice they had heard, he exclaimed:

"So, here you are, Inchester! And a devil of a job I have had in finding you!"

The Earl rose to his feet, but Lord Shaptill was already beside him.

"When I saw you at the White House," he went on, "I could hardly believe my eyes – dressed up to the nines and doing the town in style! Only a month ago you were telling me a hard-luck story that you had not a penny to bless yourself with!"

"Let me explain –" the Earl began.

"Lies! Lies!" Lord Shaptill shouted. "And damned lies at that!"

The Earl realised he had been drinking.

He tried once again to speak but Lord Shaptill shouted:

"And what do I find now? Footmen in the hall, and you eating and drinking with silver on the table! Where is your poverty, curse you! And where is the £2,000 you owe me, and have owed me for two years?"

"I know," the Earl said, "and I was going to send you

a cheque to-morrow."

Lord Shaptill laughed and it was a very ugly sound.

"Do you think I believe that?" he asked. "You are a liar and a trickster, and I do not believe a single word you say!"

He drew a deep breath before he went on:

"Poor indeed! Struggling to keep your head above water! And here you are, spending your money on some soiled dove who is doubtless picking your pocket of money that should be mine!"

"I have already told you, if you will listen to me.." the Earl tried to say.

"Listen to you?" Lord Shaptill retorted. "Why the devil should I? I have listened to your whining long enough!"

He suddenly pushed past the Earl to stand at the table glaring at Benita.

She had been listening to him in sheer astonishment.

"Pay me!" he screamed. "That is a likely story! So I will take what I can while it is available and start with this pretty 'Cyprian'. I am quite certain she costs more than you can afford!"

He put out his hand towards Benita, knocking a glass off the table as he did so.

She gave a little cry and shrank back in her chair to avoid him.

The Earl caught hold of Lord Shaptill by the arm and pulled him away from her.

"Behave yourself, Shaptill," he said, "and do not insult my wife!"

"Your wife!" Lord Shaptill sneered. "That is another lie! She is a little strumpet you found at the White House or picked up at the Coal Hole."

He spat out the words.

But the Earl, with the punch of an experienced pugilist caught him a blow on the chin that knocked him to the floor.

"Get out of my house," he said, "and do not dare come here again insulting my wife! A cheque, with interest, will be sent to you to-morrow!"

Lord Shaptill glared at the Earl from where he had fallen, then slowly got to his feet.

"You struck me, Inchester, and I consider it an insult! I demand satisfaction!"

"You are drunk," the Earl said. "Go home, Shaptill. We will talk about this to-morrow but not now."

"You will fight me like a gentleman," Lord Shaptill said, "or be branded as a coward as well as a twister and a liar!"

The Earl was silent and Lord Shaptill went nearer to him.

"Will you fight me?" he demanded. "Or do I have to tell you once again that you are a coward."

"Very well," the Earl sighed, "I will fight you, but it had better be to-morrow."

"Now!" Lord Shaptill shouted. "What the hell are you waiting for, unless you intend to run away?"

"I will not do that," the Earl said grimly. "But it would be far better if you went home to bed and waited for my cheque."

"I am not going to bed unless I can have that pretty little harlot in it with me!" Lord Shaptill replied.

With difficulty the Earl prevented himself from striking him again.

Instead he said quietly:

"I will fight you, and the sooner the better!"

"I thought you would see sense," Lord Shaptill said, "and I suggest my coachman can act as Referee."

Bolton had come into the Dining-Room to see what all the noise was.

Now he came forward.

"Excuse me, M'Lord," he said, "but I acted as Referee when I was in His Grace's service to his young son, Lord Edward."

"Very well, Bolton," the Earl said, "you shall be Referee. And send for Hawkins."

"Very good, M'Lord."

Lord Shaptill had already turned to walk from the Dining-Room towards the hall.

With a cry of horror Benita jumped up from her chair and ran to the Earl's side.

"You cannot do..this! That..man has..drunk too much..and he is..very large and..over-powering."

"He is also considered a good shot," the Earl answered.

"Then please..please..do not..fight him," Benita begged. "Suppose he..hurts you."

"I will do my best to prevent him from doing so," the Earl answered, "but I am not having anyone insulting my wife!"

Benita put her hand on his arm.

"That does not..matter," she said. "Please.. please..refuse to do..what he..wants."

"You know I cannot do that," the Earl replied.

There was a twist to his lips as he added:

"As he said, I have to behave like a Gentleman!"

Benita clung to him.

"You will..be careful..very..very careful!" she whispered.

"I will," he answered, "because you have asked me to be."

He turned and walked towards the Gun-Room which

led off the hall.

There was a pair of duelling-pistols there which had belonged to his father, who had, the Earl knew, once won a similar encounter.

He could only hope that he would be as good.

He had always disliked Lord Shaptill.

At the same time, he was the only one of his neighbours who had cattle to spare and ewes when he was trying to improve his farm stock.

He had not forgotten the £2,000 he owed him.

It was one of the first debts he had intended to settle as soon as he was able to write a cheque.

It was just unfortunate, he thought, that Lord Shaptill should have seen him in the White House wearing Anthony's clothes.

He must have looked to Shaptill like all the other rich young men who gambled and enjoyed themselves with the 'Cyprians'.

He was checking the duelling pistols when Hawkins joined them.

"Now, wot's all this about, M'Lord?" he asked.

"I have to fight a duel, Hawkins, and I can only hope that I do not disgrace myself."

"Now Your Lordship be careful of that there Shaptill," Hawkins warned. "A nasty reputation 'e's got."

"What do you mean by that?" the Earl asked.

"I've 'eard stories 'bout 'im in the past,' Hawkins replied. "'E's not a stickler for the rules, an' shoots too 'igh or too low, so they sez."

The Earl thought he had heard that particular story himself.

"Well, there is nothing I can do except hope that I am quicker on the call of ten than he is."

"Then jus' watch your step with 'im, M'Lord,"

Hawkins said ominously.

They went from the Gun-Room out into the hall.

Benita was waiting there.

Because by this time most of the household knew what was happening, Nanny had come downstairs.

She had a fur cape to put over Benita's shoulders.

Lord Shaptill was already going down the steps.

As the Earl followed he realised Benita was beside him.

"You are to stay here," he said sharply. "You are not to watch."

"Of..course I am..going to watch!" Benita answered. "And please..please..do be..careful!"

The Earl was just about to argue with her.

Lord Shaptill had however reached the level grass lawn just in front of the house.

"Are you coming, Inchester," he shouted, "or are you still acting the coward?"

The Earl pressed his lips together to stop himself replying.

Instead he walked slowly and silently to join Lord Shaptill.

Then they were both standing in front of Bolton with their pistols in their hands.

CHAPTER SEVEN

"One – two – three – four – five –"

Bolton was counting in his slow, pontifical voice as the duellists walked away on either side of him.

With the full moon overhead and the lights from the windows it was as easy to see them as if it had been midday.

Standing on the steps, Benita was praying desperately that the Earl would not be hurt.

She thought Lord Shaptill was not only drunk but the most revolting man she had ever seen.

She was terrified when he turned on the count of ten of what he would do to the Earl.

She was praying that he would shoot wide.

"Seven – eight – nine –" Bolton said.

Before he could even finish enunciating the word 'nine', Lord Shaptill swung round and fired.

As he moved and before he had actually pulled the trigger Benita screamed.

The Earl instinctively turned sharply towards her.

His foot slipped.

The bullet which was intended to hit him in the back and either kill or cripple him just grazed his left arm.

As he heard the shot he instinctively fired his own pistol.

Lord Shaptill was now facing him and the Earl's bullet caught him in the shoulder. He staggered and fell to the ground.

Benita had eyes only for the Earl.

She ran down the steps and flung herself against him.

"He..cheated! He..cheated!" she cried. "Are..you all..right? You..are not..hurt?"

The Earl dropped his smoking pistol on the ground and put his arm around her.

She looked up at him, her eyes wide with fear.

She looked so lovely in the moonlight that without even thinking he bent his head and kissed her.

For a moment they were locked together.

Benita felt as if the moonlight was seeping through her whole body.

It was a rapture and a wonder that was beyond anything she could ever imagine.

Then she heard Hawkins say, and his voice seemed to come from a long distance.

"Yer're bleedin', M'Lord, and yer'd best come straight into th'ouse!"

Benita awoke and for a moment could think of nothing but the wonder of the Earl's lips.

Then she remembered the commotion there had been last night.

It was Hawkins and Nanny who had taken charge.

They assisted the Earl back to the house so that they could tend to his wound.

Nanny had sent Benita out of his bedroom.

While they undressed him she stood on the landing above the Hall.

She could see through the windows and the open door Bolton giving instructions to Lord Shaptill's coachman.

They had lifted him into his carriage and he was being driven away.

Bolton and the footmen came back inside the house.

They told the Housekeeper and anybody else who would listen how disgracefully Lord Shaptill had behaved.

He had cheated and might have killed the Earl.

"But..he is..alive!"

Benita wanted to shout the words aloud for the sheer joy of knowing it was true.

Now the sun was shining through the sides of the curtains.

When she looked at the clock she was astonished to see how late it was.

Then she remembered that Nanny had given the Earl what she said was a "soothing drink".

She had then taken her to her room and helped her get undressed and into bed.

"I want to see His Lordship and say good-night to him!" Benita protested.

"His Lordship's asleep now, and that's what you'll be in a few minutes."

There was no use in arguing.

Nanny gave her some of the soothing herbs and insisted on her drinking them.

Benita had fallen asleep without seeing the Earl, and had slept without dreaming all through the night.

"I will see him now!" she thought.

She was suddenly afraid that the wound had proved

worse than they had thought.

Perhaps he had lost so much blood that he was weak and ill.

She got out of bed and put a pretty blue satin negligée over her nightgown.

She was however not thinking of anything but the Earl.

She knew she must reassure herself that he was still alive.

She went from her room into the corridor.

Knocking gently on the door of the Earl's room she received no answer.

Afraid of what she would find, she opened it.

The curtains had been drawn back, and the Earl was not in his bed.

He was sitting in the sunlight in one of the windows.

Because Benita was so glad that her fears were unfounded she gave a little cry and ran towards him.

The Earl did not rise but held out his hand.

"Benita!" he exclaimed. "I was told you were still asleep."

"Are..you all..right? You are..not ill? You..are not in..pain?"

The questions seemed to tumble from her lips.

The Earl smiled.

"Thanks to Nanny and Hawkins I slept like a log. My wound is only a scratch and does not even hurt me."

Benita drew a deep sigh of relief.

"That terrible, wicked man..tried to kill..you!"

"Forget him!" the Earl answered. "The story of his bad behaviour will be all over the County soon and I doubt if he will show his face for a long time."

"And you are..really not in..pain?"

"I might have been if you had not saved my life, as

Hawkins has never stopped telling me!"

As he spoke, Hawkins came in with his breakfast and put it on the table beside him.

"You see," the Earl said to Benita, "I am well enough to eat!"

"Mornin', M'Lady!" Hawkins said. "Shall I bring yer breakfast in 'ere with His Lordship?"

Benita looked at the Earl.

"Of course!" he answered for her.

As Hawkins hurried away to get it the Earl smiled and said:

"We have a lot to talk about, and may I say you look very beautiful in the morning?"

Benita blushed. She had forgotten she was only wearing her nightgown and negligée.

She made a little movement, as if she would rise.

"Stay where you are!" the Earl said. "Looking at you is far better for me than any medicine!"

She blushed again.

Then when Hawkins brought her breakfast she forgot to be self-conscious.

They talked not about the duel, but what they were going to do in the house.

They speculated as to what the pensioners were saying about their feast of beef and mutton.

They were still talking when Hawkins came in to say:

"Captain Dawson's 'ere to see you, M'Lord."

Benita got to her feet.

"I had better go and dress," she said a little shyly.

"Yes, of course," the Earl said, "but come back soon. I have been bullied by Hawkins and Nanny into saying I will stay in my room to-day."

Benita smiled at him.

She would have left to walk through the door into the

passage if the Earl had not said:

"Use the communicating door – it is easier."

Benita looked at him in surprise.

It was the first time she had realised there was a communicating door between their rooms.

Then she heard Captain Dawson speaking to Hawkins.

She went through it quickly and shut it behind her.

As Captain Dawson came towards the Earl he said:

"I am sorry to hear what occurred last night. It was certainly most disgraceful behaviour on the part of Lord Shaptill."

"He had some excuse for it," the Earl replied. "I do owe him £2,000, and he thought I was spending his money on riotous living!"

He looked enquiringly at Captain Dawson as he spoke who said:

"The reason I have come here to-day is to explain your financial affairs, but first I have something else to tell you."

He sat down opposite the Earl and said in a low voice:

"Major Grenfel died yesterday."

"Died?" the Earl exclaimed.

"It was what he expected, and why he wanted to make certain his daughter would be in safe hands."

The Earl did not speak and Captain Dawson went on:

"The Major told me to tell you not to let Her Ladyship know of his death until she could turn to *you* for comfort."

The Earl drew in his breath.

He knew exactly what Benita's father had meant by that.

He was sure that they were very near the point when

he would be able to comfort her.

"The Major also said," Captain Dawson continued, "that on no account was his daughter to go to his funeral, or to wear black."

"I understand," the Earl said, "but I think now, Captain, you must tell me the truth as to how and why Major Grenfel was involved with Rustuss Groon."

There was a little pause before Captain Dawson replied:

"The Major left that to my discretion, but I agree, My Lord, it is something you should know."

"Then please tell me," the Earl said simply.

"Major Grenfel and I were both wounded at the Battle of Ciudad Rodrigo."

"You were there?" the Earl exclaimed.

"We were both in the Royal Horse," Captain Dawson replied, "who suffered five hundred casualties. The Major was badly wounded, and I had a bullet in my leg."

The Earl was aware that the Battle of Ciudad Rodrigo was the 'turning point' in the War.

That the British succeeded in capturing the Fort was the first step in the downfall of Napoleon Bonaparte.

"We came back to England," Captain Dawson continued, "and were in London for the Major to see specialists, and to give a report of the battle to the War Office."

The Earl nodded.

"It was then when we visited our Clubs – the Major's being White's and mine Boodle's – that we were disgusted and horrified at the way in which the 'Bucks' and '*Beaux*', as they call themselves, were behaving.."

"Gambling and drinking," the Earl remarked.

"Exactly!" Captain Dawson agreed. "It was such a contrast to the courage and suffering we had witnessed in

Portugal that the Major was incensed by it."

"I can understand his feelings!" the Earl murmured.

"While the Army was often short of food and ammunition, these young men were throwing away fortunes on the turn of a card and bankrupting themselves by going to the Moneylenders."

"What did Major Grenfel do about it?" the Earl asked.

He was beginning to see the pieces of the puzzle falling into place.

"He went to see a friend," Captain Dawson explained, "who had made a huge fortune with the East India Company and had come back to England, like so many other wealthy men, to die."

The Earl waited.

"When the Major told him what he wanted to do, his friend laughed until he choked."

"What was it he wished to do?" the Earl enquired.

"He wanted above all to provide work for the men who survived the War, and to save the estates which they had looked on as their homes from going completely bankrupt."

Captain Dawson smiled as he said:

"In order to do so Major Grenfel became 'Rustuss Groon'!"

The Earl remembered the grotesque spectacle Rustuss Groon had presented in the dingy office.

"We set the whole thing up together," Captain Dawson continued. "The Major bought a wig from a theatrical costumiers and only saw his clients by candlelight."

"I can hardly believe it!" the Earl exclaimed.

"Nobody penetrated his disguise, and I believe he became the most hated man in London!"

The Earl remembered how Sir Anthony had described

him.

"He set up an excellent spy system," Captain Dawson continued, "through this he knew exactly which client was worth saving, and which was really beyond help."

"I was one of those he saved," the Earl remarked quietly.

"The reports on how hard you worked and how much you cared about your people were very moving," Captain Dawson replied. "You must read them one day."

"And the Major made a fortune?"

"You can see for yourself," Captain Dawson replied.

He opened one of the Account Books he had brought with him and pushed it towards the Earl.

"That," he said as he did so, "is approximately the sum total of what Her Ladyship owns."

. The Earl gasped.

It was a sum that far exceeded his wildest dreams.

"You can imagine," Captain Dawson said quietly, "that the Major was terrified of her falling into the hands of one of those reckless young gamblers who would fritter away her money and then leave her broken-hearted."

"I swear to you I will do neither of those things," the Earl said solemnly.

Captain Dawson put the books and papers he carried into a pile.

"I will leave you to peruse these at your leisure," he said, "and you can pay Lord Shaptill and anybody else to whom you owe money with the Notes of Hand which are in an envelope."

"Thank you!" the Earl said.

"Now I must go back."

"You would not like to stay to luncheon?" the Earl invited.

The Captain shook his head.

"I have to arrange the funeral, and when it is over I must start to look for a home for my wife and children."

The Earl looked surprised and the Captain explained:

"I have been living in London in order to help the Major with his work. But my sons love the country, and so does my wife."

"I have an idea!" the Earl exclaimed. "And I know when I tell her about it that my wife will agree."

"What is that?" Captain Dawson enquired.

"It is that you should live at the Manor, if that would suit you. I know Benita loves the house, and if you are there she will feel she still has a personal contact with what has been her home for so long."

Captain Dawson's eyes lit up.

"Does Your Lordship really mean that?"

"My wife will have too much to do here to have any time to spend on another house," the Earl replied. "I expect she will want any personal mementoes of her mother and father but the rest is yours!"

Captain Dawson held out his hand.

"The reports the Major received about you did not exaggerate your thoughtfulness and generosity."

He walked across the room just as Benita came in through the communicating door.

"Captain Dawson has to leave," the Earl said. "But I am sure you would like to show him out."

"Yes, of course," Benita agreed.

The Earl heard her chattering gaily as they went down the passage.

He looked at the pile of papers which Captain Dawson had left behind him and put his hand up to his forehead.

He could hardly believe that his whole life had changed so astonishingly in what seemed only a few hours.

When Benita came back he knew that the one thing that mattered to him more than anything else was his wife.

She looked exquisite in the sunshine coming through the window which turned her hair to a halo of gold.

He thought there was an expression in her eyes he had never seen before.

It was time for luncheon before she had finished telling him what was going on in the house and how far the painters had got in the Library.

Then when the footmen cleared the table, Nanny came bustling in.

"Now, M'Lord," she said, "you've got to rest your arm and yourself, and no nonsense about it!"

"I am perfectly well, Nanny!" he protested.

"That wound will start to bleed again if you aren't careful," Nanny insisted, "and I'll not have Her Ladyship worrying herself sick because you'll not take care of yourself!"

Benita laughed.

"It is no use," she said. "You will have to do what Nanny says, or else she will punish you by not letting you ride *Hawk* tomorrow."

"That is something I have every intention of doing," the Earl said determinedly.

"Not unless you rests now, M'Lord!" Nanny replied.

The Earl made a helpless gesture with his hand.

Benita went through the communicating door while he took off his dressing-gown and got into bed.

"Now you try to sleep," Nanny instructed as she pulled the curtains closer to block out some of the light. "These goings on have been a nasty shock to all of us, an' nobody can deny that!"

"No, of course not, Nanny," the Earl said meekly.

Nanny and Hawkins left the room.

A few seconds later Benita peeped in through the communicating door.

"Are you asleep" she asked.

"No!" the Earl answered. "And unless you come to talk to me, I shall get up!"

"That is blackmail!" she expostulated.

"Whatever you call it, I mean what I say," he replied, "and I am bored with lying in this big bed all by myself."

She moved towards him and he said:

"Come and lie down with me. There are lots of things I want to talk to you about."

"L..lie down..with you" she murmured.

"Why not?" he answered. "After all, we are married, and even Nanny cannot deny that!"

Benita laughed.

Then she hesitated and the Earl said:

"Please, Benita, I am being very brave and doing what I am told, and I think I should have a prize for good behaviour!"

Benita turned and ran back through the communicating-door.

The Earl waited a second.

Then he got out of bed and locked the door into the passage.

His eyes were closed as Benita, arrayed in her pretty negligée came shyly back into the room.

As he did not speak or open his eyes she looked at him uncertainly for some seconds.

Then she went round to the other side of the bed.

Very gently, as if she was afraid of disturbing him, she took off her negligée and slipped between the sheets.

There was a wide gap between them, but as the Earl

still did not move she turned onto her side.

With her face on the pillow she looked at him.

He was very handsome.

How ghastly and dreadful it would have been if Lord Shaptill had shot him down as he intended.

If he had not died, he might have been crippled so that he would not be able to ride again.

She could imagine nothing more horrifying.

Then she was saying a little prayer of thankfulness because he was there.

She hoped too he would be able to ride *Hawk* either to-morrow or the next day.

The Earl opened his eyes.

As he did so he turned so that he was facing her and they could look into each other's eyes.

"You are..awake!" Benita exclaimed accusingly.

"How could I be anything else when I was waiting for you?"

He moved a little closer to her and she said:

"Be careful..be very..careful not to make..your wound..bleed."

"I am not interested in my wound," he said, "but in someone very beautiful whom I met by chance when I was out riding."

"I think it was a very lucky meeting," Benita murmured.

"If you had been frightened of meeting me," the Earl said, "I was equally terrified of meeting you!"

"And..when you..did" Benita asked.

"I could not believe you were real! That is why I wanted you to come and lie down with me. I am so afraid that if you are out of my sight I shall never be able to find you again!"

"I promise that..you will..not lose..me now."

There was a note in her voice that the Earl was waiting for.

He moved even closer as he said:

"Last night, when you saved me from that drunken swine's bullet, I kissed you. Was it the first time you had ever been kissed?"

"The..only..time."

"And what did you feel?"

There was a little pause before Benita whispered in a voice he could hardly hear:

"It..was..wonderful!"

"It was wonderful for me too," the Earl said, "so wonderful that I want to be quite certain that I was not mistaken in thinking we were both part of the moonlight, and nothing else mattered."

"That is..what I..felt," Benita exclaimed.

The Earl moved closer still.

Then his mouth was on hers.

It was a very gentle kiss as if her lips were as fragile as the petals of a flower.

Also he was desperately afraid of frightening her.

Then it was not the moonlight that swept through Benita but the sun.

It moved through her breast and up into her lips.

In a way she did not understand it seemed to burn like fire against the pressure of the Earl's lips.

He kissed her.

Then he raised his head to look down at her, thinking no kiss he had ever given before had been so ecstatic.

Then he was kissing her again.

Kissing her more demandingly, more possessively, and yet she was not afraid.

He did not know whether he moved or she did, but their bodies were close against each other's.

He could feel her quivering and knew it was the most thrilling and exciting sensation he had ever known.

"I love you!" he said hoarsely. "I love you, my darling and there is nothing in the whole world but you!"

"And I..love you," Benita replied. "I did not..know it was..love until I..thought you would be..killed and knew I..could not..lose you!"

The Earl drew her closer still.

"You are everything I ever wanted in life and was quite certain did not exist," he said. "My darling, my precious, little love, now I can ask you: 'Will you do me the great honour of becoming my wife?' "

Benita understood that this was all part of their game.

What he meant was very different from the marriage in which they did not know each other and were afraid to look.

She put out her arm to pull his head down to hers.

"I..love..you!" she said, "and I..want to..belong to you..and to be..really and..truly..your..wife!"

The Earl drew in his breath.

It was what he wanted.

Yet he could hardly believe that love had come to them both so quickly and so naturally.

It might have been pre-ordained since the very beginning of time.

"My precious! My sweet!" the Earl said hoarsely. "I adore you."

Then he was kissing her eyes, her neck, her breasts and again her lips.

He was kissing her until they were both burning in the heat of the sun.

Benita thought no one could experience such rapture and still be alive.

She did not understand but she wanted to be even

closer to the Earl and be really a part of him – so they were one.

"Love me..please..love..me..like this..for ever!" she cried.

Then as the Earl made her his there was no more fear, no more suffering, only Love.

The Love which came from God, belonged to God and which no one could ever take from them...